SUNSETTER

CURTIS LEBLANC

SUNSETTER

A NOVEL

Published by ECW Press
665 Gerrard Street East
Toronto, Ontario, Canada M4M 1Y2
416-694-3348 / info@ecwpress.com

Editor for the Press: Jennifer Sookfong Lee
Copyeditor: Shannon Parr
Cover design: Caroline Suzuki
Front cover image: Serhii Tyaglovsky / Unsplash
Front cover textures: https://unsplash.com/@martzzl (for the
digital texture on the skull's aura); https://unsplash.com/
@davehoefler (for the sunset)

LIBRARY AND ARCHIVES CANADA CATALOGUING
IN PUBLICATION

Title: Sunsetter : a novel / by Curtis LeBlanc.

Names: LeBlanc, Curtis, author.

Identifiers: Canadiana (print) 20220430802 |
Canadiana (ebook) 20220430810

ISBN 978-1-77041-690-1 (softcover)
ISBN 978-1-77852-096-9 (ePub)
ISBN 978-1-77852-098-3 (Kindle)
ISBN 978-1-77852-097-6 (PDF)

Classification: LCC PS8623.E32775 S86 2023 |
DDC C813/.6—dc23

We acknowledge the support of the Canada Council for the Arts. *Nous remercions le Conseil des arts du Canada
de son soutien.* This book is funded in part by the Government of Canada. *Ce livre est financé en partie par le
gouvernement du Canada.* We acknowledge the funding support of the Ontario Arts Council (OAC), an agency
of the Government of Ontario. We also acknowledge the support of the Government of Ontario through the
Ontario Book Publishing Tax Credit, and through Ontario Creates.

ONTARIO ARTS COUNCIL
CONSEIL DES ARTS DE L'ONTARIO
an Ontario government agency
un organisme du gouvernement de l'Ontario

 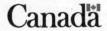

Canada Council   Conseil des arts
for the Arts   du Canada

PRINTED AND BOUND IN CANADA
PRINTING: MARQUIS   5 4 3 2 1

for Gabrielle & Marc

FRIDAY

DALLAN DERMOTT

This month of May—the hottest in memory. The oil gone and the work gone with it. Gone, too: the colour of the paint on the abandoned workyard buildings and refineries, and the green of the earth around the open gravel pit on the south side. The rusted trucks and their trailers—*Carlsbad Company* in peeling red block letters—parked again on the outskirts of Perron. This weekend, a pulse reverberating from the Sunsetter Rodeo grounds outward, and Dallan and Brooks now at the centre.

On the midway, Brooks tells Dallan that it's the black-and-yellow tent, the one with the banner that reads *Cover the Spot*. Brooks's younger brother, Aaron, filled him in. He frequents the smoke pit at school between periods, huffs white clouds among friends with similar interests. Earlier today, he told Brooks some out-of-towner came by, probably about seventeen or eighteen, and gave them a lead on where to get good, clean shit for cheap at the Sunsetter. Dallan has always supposed Aaron got his penchant for hard partying from his older brother, but the truth is that it's

9

a common pastime in any town with nothing to do and nowhere else to go for miles and miles in all directions.

Dallan approaches the black-and-yellow tent with Brooks. He's sure it's the one—how many spot-covering games could there be?

There's some commotion there now, two guys getting into it, and that doesn't bode well for their plan. There are always cops patrolling the midway and it isn't hard to pick out the jagged movements and breathy grunts of a fight about to break out.

Think something's getting busted up? Dallan asks.

Don't know. Doesn't look good, though.

They stand dead centre in the thoroughfare and watch to see how the situation unfolds. A stream of people splits around them like they're two stones in a shallow stream. Dallan is nervous. He doesn't do this sort of thing often, but Brooks tried rolling the month before and said he had a blast, that it's like the world around you is shivering with bliss and you love everyone you see, and they love you right back. The two of them did most things together, and so Brooks convinced him that the Sunsetter would be the perfect place to try it out, with the music and the lights, the rides and the girls.

It looks like it's dying down, Dallan says.

I know that guy, says Brooks. That's Travis Lent. From the team. Starting point guard, our junior year.

Travis Lent walks away from the crowd with his friends, their arms around each other's shoulders. He's probably heading to the beer tent to blow off some steam or the smoke pit for a Black and Mild.

They're about to pass by Dallan and Brooks, but Travis stops up. Brooksie, he says. He has a wide smile on his face. What's good, man?

Brooks and Trent do a choreographed handshake, the likes of which Dallan has never seen, sliding their fingers along each other's palms and bumping fists at the end.

Just hanging, man, Brooks says.

Right, right, Travis says. Who's your pet? He wags his chin at Dallan.

Dallan Dermott. He graduated with us, same year. You know him.

Right, Travis says again. Say, Brooksie, you know where we can get some tight shit tonight? Our hook-up fell through right before we came out here.

I'm checking something out in a bit. Find me later and I'll let you know if it's decent.

Cool, Travis says. He and Brooks do their handshake again, this time ending in a firm embrace.

†

By then, Dallan and Brooks had been at the Sunsetter for a couple hours. The gates had opened up at four in the afternoon, but the early hours were a little tame for them, so they stole a few beers from Dallan's place and drank them in an alley in the commercial district beside the rodeo grounds while they waited for the night to start. Once the cars started to flood the parking lot and people crowded the admissions area, they crossed the street, paid their way, and went straight for the grandstand to watch the first chuck-wagon races of the weekend.

They sat at the very top of the aluminum bleachers, going against what most rodeo-goers do, sitting as close to the action as possible. That's because, after much debate between the two of them over many years of attending the Sunsetter, Dallan convinced Brooks that this was the only spot where you could appreciate the race as a whole, the breakneck battle in every corner and the separation gained or lost in each straightaway.

In truth, Dallan knew he was the only one of them who was interested in the chuckwagons at all. It was his father's favourite event and he'd developed an attachment to it at an early age. Familiarity has always been at the root of most of his fondness, and it still gave him and his father something to talk about when he finally returned home after his long days and nights at the rodeo.

Brooks, on the other hand, had always been drawn to the excitement of an out-of-body experience, the strangeness inherent in getting fucked up or being intimate with strangers in the dark corners and the fringes of public places. He never went to the rodeo with his dad, who always took the time-and-a-half weekend shifts at Public Works that no one else wanted. Brooks's parents came from the city, and before that both had emigrated from Jamaica as kids, so the entire Sunsetter phenomenon was lost on them.

Down in the dirt arena, four wagons prepared for their first heat, each of them brightly coloured, covered in the logos of their local and national sponsors. The drivers in the front seats wore the kinds of cowboy hats that came with their own hard shell carrying cases and button-up shirts in palettes that matched whatever sponsor had been most generous to them that season. They held the reins tightly in their hands and steadied their teams of horses, four per wagon, harnessed ahead.

The chuckwagons began at the starting position, pointed in the opposite direction the race was set to go in. When the pistol fired, the drivers whipped their horses into a frenzy and guided them towards a barrel positioned ten feet behind the starting line. They spurred their teams in figure eights around these barrels and then drove them forward down the track, each horse a bottle of thunder, shaken and then uncorked by the lashing of the leather reins. Dallan watched on from the edge of his seat while Brooks slumped beside him, eyes on his phone. This was their unspoken agreement. Dallan planned the day's events and Brooks would guide them through the night.

The wagons stampeded down the first straightaway and the fastest showered his competition in a cloud of brown dust as he made gains on the first turn and again on the second. By midway, the winner of the race was a foregone conclusion. The chuckwagons made their final lap and the leader billowed through the finish line followed by the rest of the heat, all drum-like hooves and dirt and dust.

This same arena was also where they used to put on the "Cowboys and Indians" show, which was Dallan's earliest memory of controversy. It featured a prop gun shootout between chap-clad cavalrymen and face-painted caricatures that always ended in a staged massacre. This had always insulted the people from the nearby reservations and it wasn't until others from town finally joined them in a boycott that the organizers got wise and cancelled that half-baked theatre indefinitely.

All things die hard in Perron, and people protested the cancellation, claiming they were erasing an irreplaceable part of their heritage. Much to Dallan's embarrassment, his dad joined the chorus, lamenting the loss of "the only live theatre he ever liked" while the family was seated around the dinner table and Dallan stared at his broccoli and cheese sauce. Angry op-eds, anonymous hate-filled notes directed to everyone from Indigenous residents to progressive council-people alike. Finally, the local high school kids staged a walkout to end the rancor and the show stayed cancelled for good. Dallan remembers how he relished in the relative quiet that followed, but also how his impression of his father had been permanently altered, how all of his long-winded ramblings about honour or duty would forever be marked with an asterisk in Dallan's mind.

Dallan and Brooks roamed the midway for a while, eyeing up the various carnival games, knowing better than to try their hands at one, all of them slanted or bent or tampered with to give a near-impossible edge to the house. When they were younger, before they had a chance to learn from their mistakes, they would pool their money together so Brooks could shoot free throws at the basketball booth. Brooks was on the school team with Travis Lent and he had a beautiful release, a free throw percentage well above average. The carnival version appeared to them to be a sure thing in their youth, but when Brooks stood at the line, ball after ball ricocheted off the inside of the rim, out of the hoop and down onto the makeshift plywood court below.

With the first of the rodeo events holding the attention of most of the overeager attendees, the queues for the rides were almost nonexistent. Dallan and Brooks had a tradition of riding the Gravitron, a spinning top in which riders were shut in and held to the walls by nothing but centrifugal force, no waist belts or shoulder bars required. They talked the operator into keeping the ride going with only the two of them in it, at least until another patron got in line, and they stayed inside for dozens of minutes while it spun and spun, techno music thrashing from the speakers at a deafening, distorted level, as both boys tried to pry themselves from the walls with all the power their young bodies could muster.

They rode until a group of younger kids arrived and clamoured on in. Neither Dallan nor Brooks had any interest in sharing their experience so both tripped and stumbled out from the Gravitron door and down the metallic diamond plate stairs, back into the sunlight. It took them five minutes on a nearby bench to settle their stomachs and stop their heads from spinning.

Once they had regained their balance, they agreed they were finally ready. They started down the main drag of the midway in search of the Cover the Spot booth.

†

They are at the edge of the crowd around the booth. There's a guy with dirty blond hair, maybe a year or two older than them, taking money and handing out disks behind the table. Brooks and Dallan gather close behind the audience and watch as people try and fail to cover the large red spot with five metal disks.

Earlier, Brooks's brother gave them the instructions. The person who came around the smoke pit said it would be forty for two hits, that if he handed the operator at the tent the money along with a stick of chewing gum he'd get what he wanted.

It is loud and disorienting in the scrum around the booth. Two speakers strung up in the high corners play the tinny country music synchronized throughout the midway. People yell over one another, chatting with their friends or dates, and everything stinks of dust and smoke and liquor.

Brooks leans in close and cups his hand around Dallan's ear. I think we're good.

Yeah? Dallan mouths. He's used to being quiet and knows it's probably futile to try to be heard over the noise.

Brooks slips a stick of gum into his hand. Dallan takes two twenty-dollar bills from the front pocket of his jeans and wraps them around the wax paper of the gum. He clasps his free hand on Brooks's shoulder and then pushes past the rest of the onlookers to the front of the tent.

He watches as a man and a woman pay a five each to try one round of Cover the Spot. They laugh in unison and look each other in the eyes before, one after the other, they drop their disks in a circle, leaving large swaths of red uncovered. The operator shrugs his shoulders, shakes his head. He takes up the disks and tells them, Look. See. This is how you do it. He eyes the tabletop once and only once and then drops the five disks effortlessly, covering every millimetre of the bright spot on the table. Try again, he insists. You can't miss this time.

Both of them pay up for one more go at it and, again, fail to come close to replicating his effortless feat. The operator behind the table goes through his same routine, tries to tempt them into another ten bucks. The man's brow is furrowed, his intelligence and capableness scrutinized. Before he can fish his wallet from his pocket, the woman puts her arm around his waist and leads him away from the hustle. Dallan seizes his chance.

Hey man, he says. Hey!

The operator looks at him and does this thing with the disks where he spreads them out like a hand of cards between his thumb and fingers. You wanna play? he asks.

Dallan waves his hands at the disks, motioning them away, and instead places his gum stick wrapped in cash in the palm of the operator's hand.

The operator clutches his fist and seems to work his fingers over the bill. He nods at Dallan and reaches under the table. Then he says, Play a round, bud, and gives him the five disks.

Dallan takes the disks from the operator and behind the last one he can feel a small plastic pouch. He holds them between his fingers, drops them one, two, three, four, five, quick. Then he shoves the baggy in his pocket. He doesn't even look down at the table to see how he did. The operator says nothing to him as he walks away, returns his attention to the other rodeo-goers interested in his hustle.

Dallan shuffles his way through the crowd back to Brooks. He hasn't moved from his spot at the edge, standing on his toes with his neck craned. He must have been supervising Dallan through the whole exchange. Dallan has always felt like a mix between an understudy and a dead weight in their friendship, despite Brooks's patience with his social shortcomings and the enthusiasm with which he has always treated their hangouts.

You get the shit? Brooks asks.

Dallan puts his hand in his pocket and pulls out the tiny plastic bag. In it are two round white pills, nondescript save for the small round circles pressed into their centre like the outer ring of a bullseye.

Jesus, Brooks says. Put those away. He shoves Dallan's hand back towards his pants. There are cops everywhere.

Sorry, Dallan says. He shoves the bag into his pocket.

I need a beer or something first.

They know the best place to get a drink. The beer garden will charge you eight bucks for watered-down draft, but if you walk around the rodeo enclosure past the bleachers and into the forest that borders the north side—the only real greenery before the acres of dry grass that are home to the Sunsetter—you can find the bush parties where people will sell you a can or a bottle for four bucks, ice cold out of a plastic cooler.

At some point in the years prior, the cops got tired of busting up these gatherings. The partiers dispersed into the dark maze of the forest where the officers didn't have much hope of chasing them down, the coolers full of ice and beer and too heavy for them to bother lugging out of the woods to their patrol cars. Instead, the cops now focus on the pent-up rage and adrenaline of the midway, a safe bet that it will always culminate in some form of petty, bookable violence as each night wears on.

Dallan and Brooks make their way out of the crowds surrounding the amusement rides and into the relative darkness of the corral and grandstand. There are others that pass them by or follow close behind in the direction of the forest, small groups of friends talking in hushed voices, working to preserve the false clandestine nature of the bush party. Beneath the scaffolding of the bleachers, couples hold one another, kiss and whisper into each other's ears.

At the far end of the grandstand is the edge of the arena where the galvanized steel railings meet the rough stock and cattle chutes. Further still are the sorting pens where the calves and the three-quarter-tonne Brahma-crosses are kept clear of the quarter horses and broncs, palominos and appaloosas, each individual animal sorted into their own holding section before eventually being driven to the chutes at the edge of the main arena. Dallan's father used to take him there and point out all the different breeds, repeating their names so his son would commit them to memory like he had when he was his age. From inside the livestock trailers, Dallan can hear the low shuffling of hooves, their grunts and deep bestial sighs.

They continue down a clear path beginning at the edge of the woods. Already the voices and laughter of the others who have cut out for a quick, cheap beer under the cover of the greenery populate the night and hang in the cool air. The steel sound of an acoustic guitar strums in the obscurity ahead—a stereo would be too obvious, draw too much attention—and the auras of a few small campfires burn amongst the birch and spruce and poplar.

Brooks leads Dallan into one of the lighted clearings and they approach a guy with long hair leaning against the thick trunk of a tree. He wears a plaid shirt with peaked pockets and pearl snaps, and a pair of cut-off denim shorts, the white threads untrimmed and tangling with the wiry hair on his thighs. He has a white cooler at his feet with a sign made from paper towel taped to the lid that reads *BZZR* in bold black letters, drawn on in permanent marker. Brooks approaches him and hands over a bill from his wallet. The guy bends down, his long hair veiling his face, and pulls out two cans from the cooler. He reaches into the pocket of his jeans for change, but Brooks waves him off, gives him a nod, and brings the drinks back to Dallan. They tap their tops and crack the tabs.

The first time they drank together, they were thirteen. They rode their bikes out to the abandoned gravel pit where they sometimes went on the weekends or after school to poke at the remnants of the parties the high schoolers held there, empty bottles and cigarette packs and even used condoms that Brooks would pick up with a stick and then chase Dallan with.

It was a Friday. They dropped their bikes in the gravel of the workyard and walked to the pit with their school bags slung over one shoulder. The pit was dug during the oil boom, back when people from back east, the Midwest states in the south, even from as far as Mexico and Australia flocked to Perron in large numbers looking for work. The gravel that was extracted helped build the infrastructure that such an increase in population demanded: roads, concrete foundations, bricks. But eventually there was no more crude to be found in the earth, the industry dried up, and nobody needed gravel from that pit anymore. And so it sat empty and lifeless for almost as long as Dallan and Brooks have known of its existence. Now it was a place where teenagers went to drink and smoke or hook up in their cars on weekend nights, a place that the lights on the edge of town could not reach.

Earlier that day, in the morning before he left for school, Dallan's father had knocked on the door to his room and asked to have a word with him. He said that he'd found the magazines between his mattress and box spring, that he knew what they were and that they would break his mother's heart. But his father made him a deal. He told him that if he disposed of them immediately, and if he never brought the likes of them back into the house, he would not tell his mother what he'd found.

Dallan had put the magazines into his backpack, the five or six of them, wrinkled with an inconsistent gloss from years of being passed around by his peers. At lunch break, he told Brooks about his father's ultimatum. It was Brooks who suggested the gravel pit and even offered to bring along a little memorial gift for the two of them when they rode there after school.

At the edge of the pit, Dallan placed his backpack on the ground in front of him, unzipped it, and removed the magazines. Are you sure you don't want these back? he asked Brooks.

Nah, Brooks said. All used up.

Dallan held the stack in front of him, stared into the glassy eyes of the woman on the first cover. He was ashamed to look anywhere else on her body now that his father knew how he'd stashed them away in bad faith and pulled them out late into the night when his parents were asleep. He had flipped through the pages by the light of his bedside lamp until he was overcome with guilt from the uncontrollable reactions of his body.

He wound up and tossed the magazines out into the hollowness of the quarry. The pages caught on bursts of the air and fluttered apart, small inserts and subscription cards tumbling out and dispersing into the expanse. Dallan watched them fall and when he turned back to Brooks, he saw that he had opened his own bag and removed two six packs of beer held together by clear plastic rings. He tore a can off for himself and another off for Dallan and together they knocked them together the way they had seen people do in movies and sitcoms.

They stayed there all afternoon and into the night, drinking the watery smooth beer until it was gone, both of them vomiting frothy excess off the edge of the quarry after the sky finally went dark. They tried to imagine and describe the chests of the girls in the grades above them at school, gossiped about which boys were circumcised and which ones weren't. Dallan remembers how the world spun that evening, how his legs shuddered under the awkward weight of his body, and how they both walked their bikes over the unpredictable ground all the way back to Brooks's house to sleep, too drunk to ride for more than a few precarious feet at a time.

†

The quiet in the clearing of the forest is refreshing for Dallan. He has always gone to the Sunsetter out of some obligation to the severe traditions in Perron, the town he's lived in all his life. Everybody goes, as did their fathers and mothers before them, and he thinks it's true that they'll probably keep going, each day and late into the night, until the antics at sundown become too abrasive and they decide to limit themselves to the daytime races and bull riding and mud bogging like their own parents do now.

They stand and drink their beers in silence. Dallan has always been shy, had difficulties holding conversations with people whether he knew them or not. When he was a young child, he hid from adults, and when he went to school it was around the other kids that he seemed to lose all capacity for words. As a teenager, engagements with the opposite sex were completely out of the question. Brooks is the only person he's ever met who can meet him comfortably in a silence.

The pills are heavy in his pocket. Their presence fills him with

20

raw energy, a potent mix of excitement and apprehension. Brooks told him stories of rolling, how much fun it can be, how uninhibited you become, and for Dallan it's the idea of that inconceivable sensation that has been filling his mind with neurotic anticipation.

The two of them finish their beers and then agree to one more each. Dallan pays up this time on account of Brooks's empty wallet. He chooses a different vendor at the other side of the clearing, hoping for a better selection. But, like with the last guy, it's only the cheapest, most yellow beer that's available for purchase in the obscurity of the bush.

As they stand, quietly sipping at their beers, a young woman comes up to them. She places her arm around Brooks's broad shoulders and whispers something into his ear. Dallan is used to scenarios like this. They've been friends since the beginning of grade school and the moment sex became of interest to either of them was about the same time girls took a sharp interest in Brooks.

Brooks smiles at her and then says something under his breath. The two of them go on that way for a couple minutes, back and forth in low voices, and she runs her hand through Brooks's coarse dark hair. Then she kisses him, her lips pursed and tight against his. Dallan can see her hand move its way up and down along Brooks's chest. With one hand still gripping his beer, Brooks's other hand slides down between her shoulder blades and over the small of her back, and then skirts the waist of her jeans. Dallan is drunk and he watches the lashes of their closed eyes twitch as their mouths move wavelike against the other's, every now and then the curl of a tongue in the space between their lips.

The girl moves her hand along the circumference of Brooks's belt until she arrives at the buckle. She undoes the buckle and then begins to work on the button of his fly with her finger and thumb. As she pops it through its seam, Brooks flashes his hand to his crotch and guides hers away to his thigh. Their mouths come apart and they half-smile together. Brooks shakes his head. I can't leave him, he says. He eyes Dallan.

The girl touches his face and kisses his cheek, then walks away around the warm edge of the campfire, over to the long-haired guy selling beer.

Now feels right. Dallan takes the small plastic bag out of his pocket and passes it to Brooks, who pries it open and dumps the two tablets into the palm of his hand. Brooks presents them to Dallan, and he takes one between his finger and his thumb.

Roll on, Brooks says.

They toss the pills back and wash them down with the last of their beer.

The immediate rush of adrenaline makes Dallan feel like the drugs are already setting in, but in his mind he knows that's impossible. The pill is only now working its way down his esophagus, leaving a chalky white trail along the inside, soon landing in the wet mess of his stomach where it will dissolve and combine with the froth of the beer. His hands tremble and his legs feel stiff and weak, like stalks of dry straw liable to snap at any moment.

They buy another round of beer and wait for the pill to kick in. Brooks does a subdued dance, the heels of his shoes shifting in the loose dirt, and wags his fingers in front of himself along with the strumming of a nearby guitar. Dallan can feel his heart beating in his throat. He tries to chase it away with the beer, but it keeps pulsing just behind his tonsils. He clenches the arches of his feet so hard they seize and cramp, and he forces them flat again to fight off the pain.

Once they've finished off their third cans, they leave the campfire area and follow the dark path back to the edge of the forest. The glow of the midway lights up the edge of the night, a washed-out blue in the distance. As they walk behind the rodeo bleachers, Dallan begins to feel a buzzing all over like the thrum of a thousand tiny insect wings, one that makes him feel both relaxed and on edge at the same time. He wants to climb the scaffolding to the top of the grandstand and watch the lights of the amusement rides—red and blue, yellow and white—cut the night sky to ribbons.

He breaks into a short jog ahead of Brooks then spins around to urge him to keep up, to get on his level. But Brooks isn't on his feet. He is on his hands and knees in the grass. Two young women approach and as they pass Brooks, they look him over, then whisper to each other and laugh the quiet laughter that only ever comes at the expense of someone else. Then Brooks collapses onto his side.

Dallan rushes over and grabs his shoulders, rolling him onto his back. The way Brooks feels against his hands, it's like he's producing his own magnetic field. Brooks, he says. Buddy, what's up? You dizzy? You okay?

Brooks is unresponsive. His eyelids are near shut. They twitch and flitter. Dallan grabs his hand—the tips of his fingers are cold, his palms clammy with sweat. The moisture seems to only intensify the transfer of the charge he feels from Brooks's skin. Dallan takes out his phone and turns on the flashlight to try to get a better look at him. His inner lips are tinged purple. A crowd is starting to form around them. Dallan holds his face close to Brooks's to check for his breath but it's almost nonexistent, barely a whisper.

Dallan calls for help. The darkness around him spins and swirls with the lights. He is at the centre of two colliding galaxies, a constellation coming undone. He screams as loud as he can, uninhibited by the substance gripping his body and flooding his brain. More people gather around them. A young man and woman move Dallan aside and begin checking Brooks over methodically. A pair of flashlights cut through the crowd and soon two police officers are standing over them. One of them says something into his radio and the other moves to direct the crowd away.

Dallan falls back onto his hands and watches all of it unfold like a movie with poor lighting and a rushed plot. He has never felt so full of life and it makes him feel guilty with his eyes locked on Brooks, motionless in front of him. He wants to share with Brooks whatever it is making his body burst and shake, to lend him that vigor. He questions whether the source of it might actually be Brooks himself, as if Dallan has leeched the strength from his arms and legs, pinning him to the ground.

An ambulance kicks up dust as it comes around the corral on the dirt road, sirens overpowering the distant screams and music of the midway. It pulls up close to a police officer and the two paramedics rush to Brooks's side.

Dallan backs away from them, partly to give them space to work, but also to avoid watching what he can hardly believe is unfolding. His mind and body are contradictions. Both horror and joy compete to colour the scene. He makes himself part of the crowd that's locked in place, all concerned murmurs and lowered eyes. One paramedic's gloved hand checks for a pulse on the side of Brooks's neck. She holds it there for several seconds, maybe a minute, and then pulls her fingers away. The other breaks into a jog back to the ambulance.

The remaining paramedic pulls a black pouch from her waist. She removes a syringe, draws the liquid from a small vial, and stabs it into Brooks's thigh. Dallan winces and touches his hand to his own upper leg.

Immediately, the paramedic brings her hands together over Brooks's chest and pounds down with all her weight, pressing on his rib cage in a series of thrusts, more than Dallan can count, until she leans down and hovers her face over Brooks's mouth. She holds his forehead with one hand below his hairline and places the other beneath his chin. She tilts back his head and pinches his nose, then appears to kiss him gently on the lips. She does this two more times and Dallan wonders if Brooks might be enjoying it, her loveliness held above him, fully fixated on his. A tinge of jealousy even blooms in Dallan.

But when the paramedic places her hands firmly on his chest and resumes the brutal plunging motion, fear replaces all other sentiment. It drives through him like a stake into the cold earth. He is locked on Brooks, on his horrible frozen face and his half-open eyes and the hollowness of his stock-still body.

The other paramedic breaks back into the circle of onlookers with a small white case, a picture of a red heart pierced by a bolt of lightning on its lid. He opens the case and removes two pads. The first paramedic rips the plaid shirt off of Brooks's body, the buttons popping loose from their threading, and together they position the pads on Brooks's chest and abdomen. His shoulders lift. His body shudders.

While the first paramedic feels again for a pulse, the second bends down close to the screen inside the apparatus. They wait. Then he looks at his partner and shakes his head. Now, as they huddle over Brooks, their movements are slower, less urgent. One stands up and walks in Dallan's direction, stopping at the officer with his back to the crowd, arms outstretched, holding them back. Dallan sees her tell him something but he can't make out what.

There is now only a dull static on Dallan's skin, a thrum of white noise all around him. He stumbles backwards past the crowd and into the dark. Then he remembers the black and yellow tent.

EARLIER
THAT
DAY

HANNAH FIELDS

She has spent many hours of her short life waiting at the corner of Meadowview and Cochran for the traffic light to change. Evenings after her shift at the clinic, on her way home from school during the dozen years before this one, or else returning from a quick trip to the twenty-four-hour convenience store on the southeast corner of the intersection, she has learned to wait.

She stares at the red signal, but her eyes are out of focus. Her mind is elsewhere, in a place where even a sudden shift to green might not be enough to pull her back into the present. In the left turning lane, the idle engine of her car vibrates up the steering column, through the wheel, and into her hands. She is nervous for tonight, to see Nick again. It's been a year since he left and so little has changed for her here. He hasn't called, hasn't texted her in a week. What if he isn't there when the gates to the Sunsetter open in a few hours? Trust has always been a difficult balancing act for her. Nick—what she feels for him combined with his recent silence—has her threatening to fall back into a more comfortable solitude.

It's thoughts like these that have been consuming her in recent days. They've made it so she often fails to register the ringing of the landline or a knock at the door, or can't hear it when her parents call her name from downstairs or even across the dinner table. She has kept him a secret from her parents, afraid they wouldn't understand, that they would judge her for starting a relationship with someone like Nick, a *carnie*, they would call him. She's barely told anyone, shirking plans with friends and hiding in her bedroom, retreating into her conversations with him by phone or text, into thoughts of him and their possible future together.

She is clouded—though the sky is clear. The sun's white aperture is low and blinding in the horizon ahead, sitting right below the tinted strip on her windshield. It's so bright, she can't make out the driver of the pickup as it turns left into the lane beside her on an angle so wide its bumper collides with the front of her car.

The sound rips her back into reality—the pop of the headlight, the grind of warping metal, and then the shriek of the truck's bumper scraping down the side of the car as it veers right and drives away.

Only the passenger side airbag has deployed, the one on her side apparently defective—for how long, she has no idea. At first all she can hear is a constant, even ringing, but it eventually gives way to the pop and tick of her failing engine. Her eyes water and she touches the place on her neck that took on the brunt of the whipping motion as her head jerked forward then slammed back into the headrest. She catches her own face in the crooked rearview mirror. She is not hurt. She speaks to herself calmly, tells herself she is alright.

After three hard heaves against the door, it opens. The car has never been a prize, not since she bought it online off an old woman at a discount on account of the smell of cat piss that could not be exorcized from the upholstery in the back seat. Now the inner components of the headlight hang limp out of the socket and a hiss comes from under the ruptured hood. The fender, reduced to crumpled, raw metal, has caved into the now deflated tire.

It's not close to rush hour yet and there are no other drivers at the intersection. The practising physiotherapist sent her home at lunch and took over desk duties herself because she kept ignoring the patients approaching the reception desk, lost in her own anxious thoughts. She turns and looks down the road in the direction of the speeding truck. It is gone, out of sight.

She has saved almost every dollar she has made in her first year out of high school for Nick's return. They are going to need a down payment for a place of their own, some money to buy furniture and household items, and more for the precarious period when he looks for a job in Perron and she's the only one with an income. He doesn't have a college education and positions for labourers in town have been scarce for years now. In Perron, everything has felt scarce for years now. She can't afford a new car, not now, and this one is nowhere close to worth the repair cost which she knows, judging by the extent of the body damage, will be exorbitant.

She lets out a stream of curses. She has come to resent the taut anxiety of this May and longs for the soft excitement of the previous one. There was once a breathless anticipation for Nick to come back to Perron, for this year's Sunsetter and the new chapter she hoped it would bring, but Nick's silence over the past week has filled her with so much dread that the act of rising out of bed in the morning has become a labour.

And now this. Her car, the only thing of real value she has ever owned, is wrecked at the intersection with no one to blame. It was probably some guy, amped up on the first day of the rodeo and midway, already drunk in the mid-afternoon. She will probably never find out his name. She will call a tow truck, then her parents for a lift, and go on with her weekend as if nothing has changed. It's how she has always dealt with hardship, and why should today be any different. At the rodeo grounds on the west side of town, the rest of her life is waiting.

PRETTY NICK

The game looks easy enough. A red spot painted on a yellow canvas, spread tight over the top of a table inside a booth. The player gets five metal circles, each about three inches in diameter. The idea is to drop each circle from an inch above the canvas, let them go just right, one at a time, so together they cover the circle, not a speck of red showing underneath. A half-decent operator can do this ten times out of ten.

The trick is in the first two disks. You've got to drop the first one careful so the edge of the disk cuts the centre of the spot in two. It helps if you hold it with your finger and your thumb at both ends, right in the middle. The next disk goes above it, the bottom landing right above the centre of the spot. After those first two disks, it's just a matter of covering the rest. One at the bottom, one to the side. The fifth one comes down over the last splinter of red paint and you've won yourself a prize.

Players are drawn to Cover the Spot naturally. It looks easier than anything else on the midway. A good operator will play this up, call into question the capabilities of a passerby, drop the disks without looking. You get five disks, one try—it's too easy a challenge, too safe an opportunity to pass up.

Nick doesn't have to skew a thing and he'll probably still make out fine. But he has a few hustles for the guys who talk big for their girlfriends or the ones with the fat wallets who look down on him for doing what he does to make a buck.

People often accuse him of swapping the disks, dropping bigger ones himself, just for show, and then trading them out in some sleight of hand trick. It's nothing that obvious, though. The margin of error with the disks is so thin, all he has to do is step on the canvas with the toe of his shoe and stretch the red dot by a fraction of an inch, right at the moment when the last disk is falling, to get a sliver of red to show and a win for the house.

†

Nick makes his way through the campground, lifting his chin at the various other Carlsbad Gaming Company operators getting ready to raise the tents and booths for their respective enterprises. His boss Del, who oversees the operations of the dozen carnival games belonging to Carlsbad, is holed up in his Jayco camper at the end of the first row of trailers. It's just past two and Nick has an appointment with him before the midway officially opens at four that afternoon.

He's been dreading the meeting, but it's one he knows he can't miss. Every extra dollar he's made over the past year, he keeps in a Walker's shortbread tin tucked between his mattress and the wall of the trailer he shares with two other operators. This week, in the moments he's found himself alone, he's opened it and counted through the bills, the stiff creaseless ones from Del or the soft timeworn ones he sometimes gets as tips at his booth. There isn't nearly enough. He hasn't bought a pack of cigarettes in two weeks and didn't even pick up another one of the prepaid phone cards he buys at gas stations to keep in touch with Hannah. They haven't talked in over a week and he feels guilty for it, apprehensive also of what she might say when they're finally face to face again.

Nick stands at the closed door of the trailer and inspects his reflection in the weather-strip-lined window. His jaw is stiff, cheeks sallow. He runs his hand through his dark blond hair and gets it parted right. Del bought the trailer only one month before, brand new, straight from a dealer back east. He called it his twenty-seven-foot paradise on wheels and made everyone take off their boots on the AstroTurf outside before they came in. He fixed clear rubber stoppers the size of gumdrops on all of the cupboard handles to keep them from marking the face of the next door over and fitted the tips of the legs of the folding table with small felt pads.

This was before the storm a few towns back. It was only the beginning of this spring's unnaturally muggy heat, the kind that foreshadows dangerous winds and heavy rain. The clouds rolled in at late-afternoon, dark and greenish in their bellies, and from them came the largest hail Nick had ever seen, a solid twenty minutes of it. Del's paradise on wheels was permanently changed, divots the size of golf balls on every square foot of the aluminum siding.

Nick presses his thumb into one of the dents. It is so symmetrical and smooth that it almost seems it was put there on purpose, an act of Nature or of God. Then he knocks twice, loud and even, on the door.

Who's that? Del shouts from inside. He's been a rough man since Nick has known him, cusses flowing like spent air from his mouth, but he's also the most immaculate and organized person Nick has ever met, always clean shaven, hair smoothed neatly over the crown of his head with a comb, the impressions between the waxed strands of hair like those of a freshly tilled field, dark and fragrant in sowing season.

It's Nick, he answers. We have a twelve-fifteen.

The door swings outward and Del gestures him in. Pretty Nick, he says. Right on time.

Inside the trailer, there are accordion files arranged in a perfect row beside the couch and underneath the table containing the season's books, work orders, and invoices for mid-circuit top-ups on prizes. The sink is clear of dishes and no art or pictures hang from the walls. Nick has been through the cupboards and all the glasses, bowls, and plates are grouped together by size and shape, nothing ever out of place.

He sits down on the firm-cushioned bench at the kitchen table. Del comes over with a glass of water and places it before him like a gift. Nick takes a sip.

You all set for the weekend? Del asks.

Gonna raise my booth after this and then I'm ready to go. Just here to grab my float.

Good. That's good. He takes a seat across from him at the small table fastened by long triangular hinges to the wall. Sunsetter Rodeo, he says. The fucking Sunsetter! People around here go bat-shit for this.

I'm going to stick to my plan, Nick says.

Right, Del says. Business.

Nick sips from his water.

I figured you'd follow through. That's the kind of person you are. You get something in your head, and you've got no way to get it out. You've been changed since this time last year anyhow. You're a shit worker now, Pretty. Del unbuttons the top of his plaid shirt and relaxes his shoulders. It's hot, too hot. Were you with us the year this whole production nearly burned down?

I wasn't.

It was hot then, too, and parched as ever. This entire field was dried up like a big bed of tinder. It was some high school kid, piss-drunk, shot a Roman candle at the beer garden tent. It popped off the canvas and landed in some tall grass. Caught fire right quick and started spreading over the field like bright orange water from a busted sump pump. Climbed up the tent and then everyone started screaming. But before anyone got killed, rain poured from these purple clouds, so low to the ground it looked like the water might nearly bring them down, too, buckets and buckets of it. Manna from heaven. The goddamn Sunsetter.

She's coming by, Nick says. He's impatient, doesn't want to humour Del by listening to any more of his stories. I'm going to see her later today, after everything shuts down for the night.

Del smiles. Good. You're lucky—you both are. Some of us, we go through this whole death march from start to finish without ever finding anyone we can stand. What's her name again?

Hannah.

Nice name.

Nick takes another mouthful of water and swallows it down. If Nick keeps talking, Del will have to listen, get to business eventually. So I need to go through with what we talked about. I've got a little money saved, but I'll need a little more to live off of before I can find a job around here.

You gonna move in with her?

She's living with her parents.

With them, then?

I'd rather not.

No kidding. That's bad news bears, Del says. So you'll find a place?

Shouldn't have a problem. There's a lot for sale around here.

She planning on moving in with you?

I'm going to ask her. But I need enough to make a down payment and probably a little extra after that. That's why I've gotta be your guy this weekend.

Del smiles at him, taps the back of Nick's hand with a single jovial finger. You're my guy, Pretty. A promise is a promise. Let me get that float. He stands and walks soundlessly to the far end of the trailer, where his bed is made, sheets and comforter pulled tight, not a rift or wrinkle in them. He works his hands under the mattress and lifts up the end. It rises on two pneumatic arms. Nick can hear the spin and click of the safe's combination dial, the door opening and then locking up again. Del returns with a small grey lockbox in hand. He places it on the table between them with a key in the lock.

There you go, he says. That's your float for the night—plus what we talked about.

Nick unlocks the box and opens it. There are fives and tens in the slots of the money tray, plus a few twenties and rolls of change still in their brown paper wrappers from the bank. He lifts the tray. Beneath it is a large ziplock bag filled with smaller ones, each containing little white pills in singles, twos, and fours.

You move all that, Del says, and you'll have a roof over your head after the Sunsetter wraps.

Nick has never been a wild or careless person. He moves about his days with a cautious and calculated sort of foresight. When he left to join the Carlsbad crew, he did it because it was the most responsible way to get out of his hometown. Steady work, a built-in travel schedule. It was tailor-made for his vision of chasing independence. But for Hannah—he's willing to do anything to make this new life work out, in this new place with a new job and a permanent place to call his own.

He replaces the money tray and closes the lid, locks it back up with a turn of the key.

†

Nick tightens the bolts on the last of the poles that hold up the black-and-yellow nylon tent over his booth. He and the rest of Carlsbad pulled into Perron right around lunch, and after a bite with a few of the other operators—frozen burgers grilled on Del's kettle barbecue—he got right to work setting up his site. He breathes heavy from the labour, the smell of tarnished metal and damp black grease overcoming all else. Over time, the wrench has chewed a few chunks off the sides of the nuts, and he knows he'll need a new set soon. That won't be his problem if he sticks to his plan. He grips the scaffolding in two separate places and gives it a firm shake to test its stability.

Across the strip of mud and grass, more booths are being set up for the start of the Sunsetter Rodeo this evening. There are snack carts with their awnings still shut over their serving windows and food trucks with generators resting behind them, not yet churning the flat top grills and deep fryers into operation.

From his toolbox he removes a rubber mallet and a bag of stakes to secure the poles and tent corners. Corner by corner, he moves around his station for the weekend, driving the stakes deep into the soft earth through the brass eyelets on the edges of the vinyl.

One of the trucks has dropped off a folding chair and resin table and he fixes the legs straight, locks them in place, and sets it at the very front of the booth. He removes a yellow vinyl tablecloth adorned with three red circles from the bottom of the canvas bag and smooths it out on the tabletop. At the front, he pounds both corners flat with thin pegs. Around the back on his side of the presentation, he pulls the canvas down tight then finds the eyelets at each corner and drives a peg through each. They're both positioned two inches off the edge so a lip of extra material lies flat at his feet.

From pole to pole, across the front of the booth, he ties a banner that reads COVER THE SPOT in large red letters. From a bolt on one of the cross beams, he hangs a rosary of dark purple beads. He has a hunch it makes him seem like an honest person, a god-fearer to the people in the small towns they visit.

At the back of his booth, he lines up rows of toys and stuffed animals, the largest ones going at the very top. He has something for everyone: plush cartoon characters, inflatable mallets, plastic cactus cups for exotic cocktails. He's even got a few electric scooters, poorly made and built to break, that he'll sometimes give out on a slow day. The sight of another kid ripping around the midway tends to draw a crowd when nothing else will.

Finally, with a bottle of vinegar and a faded blue shammy, he wipes down the surface of the table and any parts of the tent that picked up mud in the pitching process. Then he packs up his wrench and mallet and a few loose bolts and nuts into his toolbox.

The Sunsetter Rodeo has taken place every year, long since before he joined up with Carlsbad Productions, on the edge of the small town of Perron in a large field reserved for the sole purpose of hosting the event. Save for birch forest at the northern edge of the lot, the grass of the grounds is as low and uniform as the land that surrounds the area for miles and miles. For the rest of the year, Hannah told him, it stands empty, a haven for gophers and dandelions, pot-smoking kids and off-leash dogs.

There is a large gravel parking lot for the locals and others from the surrounding county who come in for the festivities in late May. On the east side is a large tent that houses the beer gardens and sound stage and a few smaller booths for local vendors to sell handmade goods like cowboy hats and leather boots and belts. Beyond this area is the midway, where Nick has always worked, where the food vendors, carnival games, and various rides set up for operation on the Friday and are torn down no later than Monday morning when Carlsbad heads west for its next standing gig a few counties over.

When night falls on the rodeo grounds, the reek of booze and blue smoke carries down the main drag like a bad breeze. It's not unusual to see fights break out, college guys with broken noses bleeding into the dry dirt beside his tent. Nick has even watched the cops tase a few people when they tried to run off instead of spending the night in the drunk tank, the sharp prongs at the end of the guns' slinking wires flashing and sparking in the dark of the night. There are also the drugs. Pills and white powder passed between the hands of locals and visitors, peppering the seats of the outhouses and the more private carnival rides. It's never been his thing. Never bothered him that much, either. But this year is different. He's a part of it.

Across the empty thoroughfare, the last three game tents remain unassembled, their parts still in long wooden trunks and canvas bags scattered about the ground. There's the ring toss, the milk bottle pyramids, and a game for the younger kids where they fish for metallic bass with a magnetic lure. The guys in charge of them are idle, sitting on milk crates in a tight circle.

Nick smooths the cover over his table and, content with the job he's done, makes his way over to his coworkers.

Pretty Nick, one says. To what do we owe the honour?

Their faces look tired, their body language wooden and irritated.

What's up with your stations? Nick says. This thing gets going in a couple hours.

We were just talking over something fucking critical here.

Like where in this place a guy can get a fix.

You talk to Del?

We're not looking for Del's kiddy pills.

Pretty, you wouldn't get it, another says. We want to stay awake for seventy-two hours and not even feel it.

The first man draws air through his lips as if he were sucking at an invisible cigarette. We're looking for that Frankenstein shit.

I don't know about any of that, Nick says. But for fifty each, I'll put these tents up while you go into town and find it.

The three of them look at each other. They are visibly energized, their bodies reanimated.

That's a deal, one says.

Cash up front, Nick says.

Forty it is.

Fifty. If Nick let his coworkers give him shit even once, that's all he would ever get.

Fifty, the man agrees.

The three of them stand and reach into their pockets, dig out their wallets and money clips. Everyone with Carlsbad Company is paid in cash and it isn't uncommon for guys to be walking around with hundreds, if not a grand, in small and large bills. Nick collects the money and slips it in the back pocket of his jeans.

One man pats Nick on the ass before the three of them begin to walk away. Don't cut any corners, Pretty, he says. I don't want that scaffolding coming down on me.

Nick nods to them. It will take him ninety minutes to get the stations set up, a half an hour each, he figures. He gets to work.

†

The crowds are younger at first, children with their parents or babysitters. Every now and then a kid convinces his dad to fork over the five bucks to take a shot at dropping the disks and every time Nick watches them screw it up, almost always in the first two disks. When it gets quiet, Nick stands above the table and drops them himself, perfect every time, pretty as ever. This is how he reels in the people who pass his booth.

The sun has passed the centre of the sky, dipping down now into its western edge. The music gets louder and the crowds grow denser, flightier, more vulgar. Lines begin to form at the food trucks and tents where people fill themselves with blooming onions or potato tornadoes to counteract the frothy lagers consumed from red plastic cups in the beer garden or the liquor from the mickeys they've hidden in the crotches of their pants.

Nick starts marking high school guys looking to impress their dates, brings them in with the almost mystic ease at which he completes his trick. Every rational person knows it isn't that easy—how would they make any money?—but just look at Pretty Nick. Del taught Nick to prey on people's weaker parts, their insecurities and base desires. They're stupid, he said. They're animals and they'll do what you tell them to do. So long as you say it nice enough—or else you might scare them off. Nick's view of the world has never been this plainly pessimistic, but the crass nature of Del's approach has always worked. Tonight, like any night, the young men start to form a line, each guy looking to one-up the last.

Nick knows that, earlier that day, Del had sent one of the younger Carlsbad guys to the high schools around Perron. He does this in every town and city they stop in. Del's guy will approach circles of juniors and seniors in the smoke pits, spread the word about where to get a good deal if you want to roll for the night. Come by the booth with the black-and-yellow-striped tent, talk to the operator at Cover the Spot. Hand him your cash wrapped around a stick of gum and he'll hook you up, no questions asked.

Nick can't confirm this, but he's heard from the other folks around camp that the Sunsetter is where Del stocks up for the entire western leg of their tour. The supply he gets here is enough to last him the busiest six months of the year. It doesn't surprise Nick. It's the quietest places that tend to have the loudest and most troubled of sounds rumbling away, just out of earshot.

As the night wears on and the rodeo-goers get livelier, Nick pushes on the ones that look a certain way, tight buzz cuts or veins pulsing a little too hard beneath their skin. He sells to the fire-crackers and hotheads, the teens and twenty-somethings looking to make this Sunsetter an even better barstool story than the last. Soon enough, Del's little white pills fill the pockets of a hundred kids stumbling around the midway with their shirts untucked, boots muddied, and eyes vibrating in their sockets.

Meanwhile, the game goes on. A few customers get lucky and win, but that's all part of the plan. Anyone who sees them walking away with a giant stuffed gorilla or a crappy electric scooter is that much more likely to come by and take a chance.

A crowd forms around Nick's tent. He's mid-sale when he takes a five from two guys and hands them the disks. One fumbles his first two drops and it's over for him. Nick is in the middle of passing a ziplock around the right side of the table when the second guy puts a five down and takes up the disks. He drops one, two, then another, and Nick sees him go low to the table to finish his fourth and fifth.

Then Nick eyes him sliding a disk over with his thumb. He presses the pills into the hand of his buyer and turns his attention to the two he's just caught cheating.

What the fuck was that? Nick says.

The guys look at each other. Looks like I beat your disk game, bud, one says.

You think you're the first person to come here and try that?

His grin sinks into a frown. You accusing me of something?

I'm saying I saw you.

The other leans in. Just give us our fucking gorilla and we'll leave.

You aren't getting a fucking gorilla.

One steps forward and then the next. They're looming over the table, uncomfortably close to Nick. Their collective breath stinks of sour liquor. When one takes Nick by his shoulders, he rotates one of his shoulders free and slams his hand down on the stretched-out forearm of the other guy reaching for the cash. Get the fuck out of here, Nick says.

It happens at almost every stop, exactly like this. Nick catches two drunks who think they can get away with a quick slip of a disk. He calls them out and they get hot, alcohol or cocaine or whatever else pumping them up. He's become an expert at dodging sluggish, guttered fists.

Sure enough, one of the men winds up, exaggerated and lagging, to try to put Nick on his ass. But before he can swing, someone bursts through the crowd and grabs him from behind.

He's not worth it, Nick hears the newcomer say. We've got all weekend to bust some ass. They start to laugh and it is this sound, of young men howling together in a pack, that he's learned to hate the most at his job. The group walks away from the game booth, straight out of the mass of people surrounding his tent and into the throes of the midway.

HANNAH FIELDS

She can't believe it's been an entire year since she saw him here. All the sights of the Sunsetter, the colourful lights that flare and twirl in the dark sky, the smell of hot grease and sugar and turned-up soil—it brings her back, makes her remember.

The spring before, when they met, Nick was on maintenance duty. He was trying to sort out an issue with the Zipper, a tall column of pods that each spun on their own axis in a nauseating counter rotation. She was waiting in line to ride, watching him hunched over the electrical box beside the operator's booth, running his oil-stained hands again and again through his hair. Turns out Nick couldn't fix it—he confessed to her later he was worthless as a mechanic—but she watched him that entire time. His hair was blond, but with roots as dark as the grease that caked his hands, and his sparse brown facial hair was limited to his sideburns, chin, and upper lip. It gave him an appearance of being at once old and young, mature without the visible stresses of middle age. His frame was full from the manual labour he did, pointed and angled in all the right places.

Her own blond hair isn't far off from Nick's, but it's always been dull and full of static. Hannah's mother assured her that she lived up to all the conventions of beauty, pale and tall and thin, but her father often told her she was "all arms and legs" and that was the comment that rested in the back of her mind like a splinter of self-consciousness.

When Nick announced to the line of patrons that the Zipper wouldn't be starting back up after all, she made sure to ask him any and all questions that came to mind. What was the issue? How does that even happen? What all did you try? His answers were lacking, but it didn't take him long to catch on to the fact that she wasn't actually interested in his work or why the ride wouldn't start.

The two of them continued to talk as she followed him from job to job, the radio on his hip crackling out the locations of other mechanical failures and unsightly spills. While Nick worked away, she would lean on the fence that blocked off whatever ride they were at and chat him up. He was a person of few words, but the more she pressed him the looser he became and the more he started to share.

He'd been with the Carlsbad Gaming Company for two years, had joined up right after he graduated high school at the age of seventeen. He was from out east, further in any direction than she'd ever been. It was hard for him to see school through, but he finished for his mother. He wanted to travel, or at the very least leave home, so when he saw the ad for a general labourer with Carlsbad posted on the bathroom wall of a music venue back in his hometown, he ripped it down, pocketed it, and made the call the following morning.

She had always pictured herself alone and this had been acceptable to her. Being with someone meant relying on one another and with that came the potential for a kind of disappointment she never much wanted to taste. She had seen it in her mother, in the way she seemed to despise her father for his ongoing series of small mistakes: drying out a hundred dollars' worth of brisket on the backyard smoker he never learned to use, losing the keys in the crack between the floor and the elevator door at work. She had also witnessed her mother act like the girls she knew at school, reliant on their male appendages, either performing or truly believing that they had become helpless on their own. Hannah was adamant she would never rely on anyone—especially not some boy—to help her get by.

In Hannah's mind, though, she could see the beginnings of a new picture forming, one that offered her independence in a place she couldn't see herself ever leaving, with a person, this outsider, of few words and a warm sincerity. In Perron, a town she knew as well as anywhere or anything, he would have to lean on her more than she would ever have to lean on him.

That first night, after the amusement rides had finally come to a halt and all the booths and food vendors had closed up, Nick brought her back to the collection of camper vans and trailers where the Carlsbad crew stayed. He told her he was working on moving up out of maintenance, that he wanted to be on games duty instead. A man named Del was in charge of that part of the operation and Nick was in the process of getting on his good side. He took her to Del's trailer and a group of them played cards around the dining table until early in the morning. Del struck her as a sweet talker, a man who was used to getting what he wanted through the wielding of his own cleverly chosen words.

When the night was over, Nick walked her to the road that led straight through the heart of Perron back to where she still lived with her parents on Madonna Drive. She told him that she would be graduating that spring, that she'd never had a night quite like the one they'd just shared. He kissed her on the forehead, and she walked off down the road towards the faint morning light. But she did not stay away.

On the Saturday morning, she found him at the beginning of his shift. She kept him company again while he completed his various duties, greasing machinery, resupplying the various food vendors and games booths, mopping up vomit from the walkways and ramps surrounding the carnival rides, and when he finally hit a lull long enough to step away and take a break, she took him to the mud bog track beside the corral and grandstand.

Mud bogging might have been unique to the Sunsetter—she wasn't sure—but Nick didn't think he had heard of it. The two of them took their seats on a set of small bleachers to watch the souped-up Buicks and rusty half-tonnes race down a hundred-metre straight-away, three feet deep with thick mud. He was slack-jawed, amazed by the ludicrousness of the display.

There were several kids standing on the bottom beam of the shoulder-height chain-link fence to get the best view of the drag race. This also meant getting a face full of muck each time a driver in the left lane came off the last hump and met the ground again in the soupy landing pool. Their t-shirts and faces were spattered with brown mud.

Before the race, two single-cab pickups—a Ford and a Chevy—revved their engines at the far end of the bog. A rodeo clown in canvas chaps and a derby hat coaxed the crowd into applause.

That's my cousin out there in the Silverado, Hannah told Nick. No way he doesn't beat that rust bucket.

The Ford? he asked.

Stands for Found On Road Dead.

The clown pulled out a fluorescent orange starter pistol and waved it in circles through the air. The crowd erupted. Then he turned to the drivers, worked up the crowd from right to left, and fired off a blank. The tires of both trucks spun out at the starting line, sending waves of brown mud through the air behind them. The Ford found traction first and lurched forward down the dip. The Chevy followed in the lane closest to them. Their tires chewed up the soft ground and shot chunks of dirt several feet back, creating rainbows in all the shades of the deep earth. The sound of their engines and their deleted mufflers was deafening.

Both trucks were neck and neck, coming down the track. But just as the Chevy was fishtailing its way to the foot of the final hump, a big cough of blue-black smoke blasted out behind it and the truck slid through the thick mud to a halt. The Ford ripped past, over the hump and into the pool, splashing the audience on the far side of the track. It fishtailed through the caution tape finish line.

†

The Carlsbad crew spent the Sunday evening packing up the midway into trailers, leaving the rodeo grounds a mess of mud and truck ruts and trampled yellow grass. Like the two days before, she accompanied him to each of his duties, but the talk was sparse now, stifled and precious with his departure looming. In the end, he walked her home again and they repeated their ritual at the foot of her driveway. They promised to talk every day, by any means available or necessary. He kissed her head and she walked backwards up the walkway until, at the last possible moment, she had to turn and go inside.

She shut the door, careful not to wake her parents, and then slumped down against the other side. She cried into the hem of her shirt. Never in her life had she wanted so badly for the next day to work out differently. She wanted him to stay, but she failed to find the words to ask him just as he had failed to answer her silent request. She would have to wait.

Through the months that followed, she graduated high school and got her job as a receptionist at the local massage therapy clinic. She started to save for a future she envisioned with Nick. Every couple of weeks she would get a text after he'd picked up a new prepaid phone card at a convenience store somewhere along the road. They exchanged messages during the day and in the evening he would call and they would often talk into the early morning, Hannah sometimes dozing off mid-conversation and waking up with the phone stuck to her cheek. He was mostly reserved and obtuse as she had expected boys to be, but he occasionally surprised her with an emotional sincerity that reminded her what they felt was real. Once he sent her a photo of a robin's nest built under the open hood of an abandoned car, the chicks huddled amongst the remnants of their blue shells, mouths open and awaiting their next meal, accompanied by the words *thought of home, thought of you.* Through their calls and texts, Hannah and Nick hashed out plans for their future together and agreed that, the following spring when he returned, he would remain in Perron. They would do whatever they had to to make it work. The next Sunsetter would be his last with Carlsbad.

This past week, though, the last phone number she had for him went out of service, as the robotic operator told her when she tried to call after receiving no reply to several of her text messages. She had not received a new contact from Nick, no word on when he would arrive in town, and this seven-day silence was near-unbearable to her. It angered her that Nick would be so murky that close to their reunion, so aloof after a year of constant communication, a year of wanting and waiting to be together again. It concerned her, too, that something could have happened to him. Each time her phone rang over the course of the week, she looked at it with equal parts frustration, excitement, and fear, but it was never his voice that answered hers on the other end of the line.

Her nervousness has manifested itself in her body all week, a strain in her shoulders, a queasiness in her stomach, a hesitance in her step. Tonight, she's come to the grounds alone, not in the mood to enjoy the Sunsetter in the same ways she has in the past, with girlfriends from school or maybe even one of the boys who'd asked to take her there on a date. With her car in the repair shop, her father dropped her off at the foot of the parking lot, patted her cheek, and told her what he always did. *Don't be late.*

Now she's back at the rodeo grounds—and somewhere in the maze of tents and giant spinning metal tops, Nick is, too.

DALLAN DERMOTT

He feels as though all the air has been sucked from his lungs. Almost all sensation has drained from his body. He has become the centre column of the Gravitron, the walls circling around him at breakneck speed, and on each and every one of the sliding black vinyl backrests is Brooks. Brooks in the desk next to him, reaching over to show him how to hold his pencil the first day of kindergarten. Brooks in the sleeping bag beside him as they talked about the small victories they craved as boys, a car to drive and a full beard by twelfth grade and a significant other to be close to and confide in. Brooks with his hand on Dallan's back as it convulsed with his crying, when his father struck him for the first and only time after he cussed out his mother for forbidding him from attending the grade seven graduation party at Nadine Beck's. Brooks with marinara sauce clinging to his moustache in the high school cafeteria. Brooks, next to him in his bed, drunk and alive only a few weeks ago, telling him about the person he imagined he could be if only he got it through his head that he was good, that he could be good if he tried and tried again. And Brooks, hazy and half-formed, in some future whose impossibility was only now becoming apparent to Dallan.

He stands. With newfound purpose, he walks back towards the midway, his steps quick and heavy. There is a warmth building in the back of his neck, slowly flushing his ears and face. His fingernails dig into his palms as his fists clench. Inside, he is ablaze.

He comes around the Ferris wheel. He pushes past the few patrons waiting for a chance to cover the spot, eyes locked on the operator with his bony cheeks and blond hair. When he reaches the folding table with the spotted surface, he lifts one side and shoves it back into the operator's waist. He storms into the tent, takes two long strides and grabs the operator by the shoulders, then pushes him through the vinyl flaps at the back of the booth.

What the fuck do you think you're doing? the operator says.

Behind the tent, the groaning engine of the Ferris wheel is thunderous. He can smell the grease, the diesel exhaust, the air like hot metal.

Dallan chokes through a dry sob. His breath is so shallow and quick that he can feel his chest deflating. He gasps for air. He stares into the face of the man in his grip. His eyes are hidden beneath the shadow of his brow. Dallan lifts him into the light.

HANNAH FIELDS

She knows where to find Nick. Before he went quiet, he sent her a photo of his game booth from a few events back, yellow and black stripes marking its peaked roof. She locates the main drag of games and vendors and spots the Ferris wheel rolling like a circle of blue embers on the right of the thoroughfare. His booth should be below it.

Her heart quickens and her mouth dries out as she makes her way through the crowd to the end of the drag. There are no distinguishable features on the faces that pass her by, no words to make out in the discord of the midway.

Nearly at the tent, she stops and straightens her dress. She doesn't normally dress in anything but jeans and a t-shirt and is unsure how to feel in the loose fabric hanging off her high shoulders. She walks forward, her eyes nervous, counting the slow steps of her white tennis shoes. She looks up from her feet. There is no one inside the booth, only a small crowd around it speaking in a collective hush. He isn't there. Nick isn't there.

So she waits. There is a lineup at the booth but as a minute passes, then another, they begin to wander elsewhere. As the crowd around Nick's tent trickles away, so does the optimism that had pushed her down the midway to this point. She stands off to the side, eyes locked on the back entrance of the booth, aching for a pair of hands to come and part it and reveal the person she has waited the longest year of her life to see again.

No more waiting, she reminds herself. She looks around to see if anybody is watching, then sneaks around the side of the tent to look for him. It's dark between the canvas booths and she can smell the damp mould, their walls redolent with must. She's careful to step over a bundled nerve of electrical cords and then emerges into the area behind the tents.

The noise from the machinery of the Ferris wheel is overwhelming. The lights rise and fall above her like small blue planets in perfect orbit around a fixed centre. It reminds her of the night she watched Nick try and fail to fix the machine for an hour that previous May, tools littered all around him as he cussed and fumbled with its switches and valves and wires.

And then she sees him. At least, she thinks it's him. She can almost make out his shape past a set of large rubber wheels powering the ride around. His back is turned to her and it's dark behind the tents, but his hair reflects the lights of the ride above him. The blue bulbs cast him in an unnatural glow. She wants to run to him and hold him, fill his face with warmth and colour.

She's sure it's Nick—and he's not alone. There's another man with him. As she approaches, this other person becomes clearer. She recognizes him from her graduating class. It's someone she hasn't seen since school ended, but she can remember him through a small, kind gesture he made in their home economics class. From the part of her mind reserved for useless high school memories, she recalls him fixing the pasta maker attachment onto her mixer after she tried and failed to get it to work for the first fifteen minutes of the period.

He's arguing with Nick, his chest out and fists clenched, face pulled into a long scowl. They open their mouths wide at each other, barking over the staggering noise of the Ferris wheel. Nick pushes the boy and he stumbles back into one of the large metal support beams behind him. She tries to call out to them, tell them to stop, but they can't hear her over the thrum of the Ferris wheel engine.

The boy from school stands back up and pushes Nick. He trips over something behind him. As he loses his balance, his arms reach out in front of him as if trying to grasp an outstretched hand or an invisible rope. He falls backwards, out of sight. The other boy stands over him, waiting with his fists in front of him for Nick to stand back up and meet him.

Hannah draws nearer. Nick doesn't move. He stays there on the ground at the other boy's feet. Hannah rushes past the Ferris wheel's engine. The other boy drops his guard and sinks to look at Nick. He crouches beside with a hand on Nick's chest. Nick's eyes are wide open, reflecting the blue lights churning above him.

She tries to make sense of what has just transpired. She looks at her hands and they do not register as hers. It's dark save for the strobing of the coloured bulbs that line the spokes of the carnival ride circling above them. They illuminate Nick's blank face like the taillights of cars passing through the sky. The noise from the machinery washes over her whole body like hot air.

The other boy raises his head and finally registers her. She closes her mouth and swallows. Her mind tries to take in the entire scene, all at once. The two men low in front of her blend together, a double vision. She shuts her eyes and feels tears collect in their corners.

She bends down to get a closer look at Nick. His eyes are open and lifeless. They stare beyond her at the space above them. He can't be. There is a puddle of dark liquid forming around his head and she dips two fingers in, pulls them close to her nose, so much so that they rub wet against the tip. She smells the tin of blood. He isn't. He can't be.

She thinks that if she can just hold her eyes open long enough, Nick will cough and come to life like a young hero in a movie, pulled from the eddying pool of a dangerous river. Her eyes sting and she blinks them shut and then opens them again to find Nick still on his back, face empty, silent, motionless. Her tears fall and dot his dry cheeks.

Hannah runs her fingers through Nick's hair and she touches his face. He can't be. She looks up at the other boy, standing over them now, and attempts to speak. She can only move her lips, her tongue, forming the soundless syllables of the words that fail her.

The other boy bends down beside her and he too touches Nick's face. She doesn't know why he does this. It angers her. He shouldn't be touching him. He runs his finger along Nick's bottom lip and grabs his wrist, then drops his arm, heavy.

Hannah blows her nose into the hem of her dress and wipes her eyes with one hand. What did you do? she says. Why did you do this?

I don't know, the boy says. I didn't mean to. I—I . . .

Is he? she asks him.

The boy nods.

She bites her lip to keep from crying. I know you, she says.

Hannah, he says.

Her chest sinks at the sound of her own name.

It was an accident, he says.

She stares at him. He is poison in the last pool of freshwater in a desert.

Brooks, he says again. He's dead. He points to Nick. He sold it to us. It killed Brooks. That's why I came back. He killed Brooks.

She looks at Nick and begins to cry again, harder now. She coughs on the mucus running down her throat. Her nose runs down her upper lip and she wipes it with the back of her hand. Nick is here but he is not. His youth strikes her, betrays the cool confidence he used to embody. None of what makes a man out of a boy has had the chance to happen to him yet.

I didn't mean it, Dallan says. He pushed me and I pushed him back. I didn't mean for him to fall.

Hannah keeps her focus on the ground, on Nick, as if he is the one that is speaking to her, as if she can still hear him.

I'm high, Dallan says. I'm fucked up. I don't know what to do. But we need to get help.

Hannah sniffles. She nods.

Don't say anything about what happened. I'll turn myself in. I promise. I just need time to think. I need to clear my head.

She has trouble making sense of this young man's face, of the space around her. She trusts nothing, not even the image of Nick below. Her mind still tells her over and over: he can't be, he can't be.

I promise I'll make this right, he says. I swear to god. You just can't say anything yet, okay?

After a moment, she raises her head, her chin dimpled and trembling. Alright. Okay. She gasps for air. She isn't even sure if her words are audible.

Get help, he says. I'll make this right. I promise.

She takes him in through her tears. He rises up and takes off running, the horrible blue lights bleeding and weeping in the darkness around them, all the noise of the Sunsetter coming to a deafening peak, to an undividable wave.

SATURDAY

DALLAN DERMOTT

He wakes to a band of sunlight on his face, blazing through the crooked blinds of his bedroom window. He hunches his shoulders and slides his head off the pillow and under the covers, stopping with the edge under his nose. From there he watches the dustmotes pass through the beam like tiny animals, wild and desperate, darting across highways of pure light.

The room is thick with the night's heavy breath. His arms and legs are rigid and leaden, each sinking into the pillow-top mattress, and the single sheet that covers him sticks to his skin. He closes his eyes tight to try to wet them, to remove the itch from their corners, and rolls over to check his clock. It is still early and he considers going back to sleep. Then he remembers. All at once, he is anxious, alert.

He sits up and rests his head and neck against the cool wood of the headboard. The first option that occurs to him is to stay in his bedroom forever. He can take food and water through a small opening in the door and remain there until he is dead or taken against his will to a prison or an institution of some kind. The other possible course of action is to gather some essentials in a bag, steal his parents' car from the garage, and drive far enough north to where the land is wooded and wild and would allow him a life of prolonged anonymity.

But these are not acceptable options, not to him. He remembers something his father often said to him: the Dermott men have always been martyrs. His father had served on every school board and canvassed door to door for the Knights of Columbus, the Kidney Foundation, and every local politician he ever planned on voting for. Dallan had heard the story dozens of times—of his great grandfather losing both big toes to frostbite while completing his deliveries of feed, as promised, to the surrounding livestock farms during a record-breaking snowstorm. It seemed the Dermotts had always been connected by nature or blood or some other unnameable force to the duties they had invited into their lives and would do anything short of kill themselves to make good on them.

Dallan can see the girl in his head, Hannah, slouched over the young man's body, how she heaved for each breath as she cried, and he feels this same innate sense of duty towards her as he does to Brooks and his memory. He can see the face of the man he killed, better now even than in the act of killing.

It's this image that will define him now. He is a killer. This truth still feels hollow to him, but he knows what he did, that it actually happened, that it wasn't some imaginary scene drawn up by the drugs or the disorienting thrall of the rodeo. He's seen killers online, on shows, and in books. They do not look like him and he can't envision them thinking or feeling in the same way he does. Maybe some of them were normal, too, before they found themselves backed into a corner, before they pushed too hard or reached too far into the dark.

He sits all the way up in his bed, plants one foot and then the other onto the carpeted floor. He exits his room in stiff, almost injured steps. The house is quiet. There is a parade for the Sunsetter each year on Saturday morning and it's his parents' tradition to attend with his aunt and uncle. He goes to the washroom and takes a lukewarm shower, towels himself off, and locks eyes with his reflection in the mirror. He feels detached from the body staring back at him, less of a reflection, more a portrait of another person altogether.

In his room, he searches his closet for his brown chinos and a short-sleeved button up shirt. A confession—it seems to him something that requires a degree of formality, and so he supposes he should look half-decent while doing it. When he is clean and dressed and the remnants of the night before feel like they've been temporarily rinsed away, he goes downstairs. He has no appetite for breakfast, passes straight through the empty house to the front entrance where he puts on his cleanest pair of shoes.

The elm trees outside his house were planted when Mission Avenue was first paved, one of the first suburban residential roadways in town, and they've since grown into a hulking canopy along the boulevard. They converge in a grove above the asphalt, providing permanent shade to cars and cyclists and pedestrians. Their seeds have begun to drop and cover the sidewalk and the hoods of vehicles with thin, papery confetti, as if the world is throwing him some kind of sick party for doing what he did.

The police station is only a short walk away. The sidewalks and streets are quiet for Saturday morning. The rodeo has all of Perron concentrated in one place at a time: Main Street, where the parade makes its way from the Catholic church on the hill, over the river, and past the park surrounding city hall. Folks will now be starting to make their way to the rodeo grounds for the competitive events: bull riding, calf roping, and chuck wagon races. Then later still it will be the midway and large tented pavilion where people go to drink and hear the country and classic rock cover bands play.

He makes a left at the corner onto Main Street. Reality returns to him in ripples, in waves. The lucidity turns his stomach. He bends over and vomits into a hedge at the foot of a yard. The remnants of the parade—candy wrappers and popped balloons and coffee cups for nursing hangovers—line the boulevard gutters where families sat in lawn chairs and watched the clowns and bands and corporate floats stream by. There is a cold sweat on Dallan's chest and the back of his neck. He wipes his mouth with his hand and then squats to clean it off in the grass. He does not raise his eyes to meet those of the drivers who pass him occasionally. Instead he looks above them, to where he can see the three flags flying at full-mast in front of the police station at the intersection of Meadowview and Main.

He approaches the door and presses the wheelchair button on the wall. Inside, he makes his way to the administrative counter. His legs feel as if they are gliding across the linoleum floor, a sort of vehicle for the rest of his body over which he has no control. There is a woman sitting behind a thick plexiglass shield with a slot at the bottom to exchange documents or money. This is where people come in for criminal records checks or to claim their lost wallets or even, he assumes, to turn themselves in.

What's the reason for your visit? she asks. There is a hole smaller than a baseball in the glass, roughly in line with the height of her face.

I'd like to report a crime.

Is this an emergency?

No, he says. He swallows. Then: Yes.

Is it or is it not an emergency?

Last night, he says. There was an accident.

Are the police aware of this incident?

I'm not sure.

Was this incident violent in nature?

I don't know, he says. Kind of. In a way.

Is anyone in any immediate danger?

Yes, he says. They were.

The woman behind the counter raises her eyes to meet his. She must have seen his guilt then, he thinks, because she immediately calls some kind of code into the radio velcroed to the shoulder of her vest.

A solid metal door opens to his left. An officer emerges, older looking with male pattern baldness and the suggestion of a gut held tight by his tucked-in khaki shirt. He approaches Dallan and stops, uncomfortably close.

Come with me, the man says.

Dallan can smell the coffee on the officer's breath, can feel it on his face. He follows him through the metal door and into a room sectioned off into cubicles, surrounded by a series of closed office doors. There are men and women in half the workstations. Their heads are down and none look up when they enter the room and the officer leads Dallan to one of the doors on the right, marked with the number four.

Long fluorescent tubes glow harshly from the ceiling, left uncovered possibly after a routine cleaning. There is a table with two chairs on either side and a mirror that makes up half of the wall to his right. He knows it's a two-way mirror, that detectives with pocket protectors and notepads are looking on from the other side. It's almost comical to him how much it all resembles the archetypal interrogation rooms in movies.

Have a seat, the officer says, blunt, almost annoyed. Someone will be with you shortly to record your complaint.

It's not a complaint, Dallan says.

Whatever you want to call it, the officer says. He begins to leave the room.

Dallan can't stand it, how they seem to be brushing him off, how they won't take him seriously. He slams his hands down flat on the surface of the table in front of him.

I killed someone.

The officer stops at this. He turns to look at Dallan and then lets out a deep breath from his nostrils, one that rattles the hairs of his grey moustache. Without a word, he turns and leaves.

Dallan did kill someone. The truth of it burns inside of him, a bile searing his stomach. That young man is the only person he will ever kill and he wants to be heard, to be respected while he trades his life away in the name of honesty, of duty.

His hangover has made the entire world around him surreal and his thoughts respond accordingly. He runs his hands over his eyes, down his cheeks and past the corners of his mouth. Brooks is dead and so is this other stranger, a person not much older or different than himself. He didn't know him, but he was important to someone, enough so that she wept into his dead person's shirt. This is enough to make him nauseated again. He's afraid he might throw up, but all of a sudden the heavy door to the room opens back up. He swallows the spit from his mouth and washes the acid back down from the cusp of his throat.

This time it's a man in dress pants and a white shirt who enters. He wears a deep burgundy tie with a western design through the middle, two horses galloping away from what appears to be a gale of dust and tumbleweeds. He takes the seat opposite and rests his elbows on the table, chews the inside of his lip and then runs a hand through his hair. His face is smooth, almost boyish, save for the dark underscores beneath his eyes and the beginnings of crow's feet at their corners.

So my colleague tells me that you're here to confess to some kind of murder?

Dallan shudders at the word. The man's voice is clear and measured.

You don't look like you killed anybody.

I did.

Stray cats don't count.

He was working at the rodeo. This guy.

66

The detective leans in.

I don't know him. He had blond hair, I remember. We got into it and he pushed me. I pushed him back. He—he fell. There was all this blood around his head.

Was there anyone with you? the officer asks, a tense quickness in his voice that wasn't there when he first spoke. Did anyone else see this happen?

Dallan opens his mouth but stops abruptly. Something inside of him persuades him to lie. No. Nobody saw. It was just me and him.

The officer across the table stares at him, purses his lips. Then he stands and walks back out the door.

DEPUTY ARNASON

He leaves the interrogation room without so much as turning back to side-eye the young man. He cuts across the office between the cubicles, stopping at the water cooler for a drink from a waxed paper cone. The night before was a long one, reviewing paperwork and taking statements from the officers who came across the first dead kid—and then the next one. The entire evening that old rule kept playing in his head, that bad things come in threes, and he half-expected a third person to turn up dead before the clock struck midnight. He's able to do most of his work with the sense of detachment that his profession requires, but the night before was made from the stuff he remained purposely ignorant of when he first decided to join the police service.

He continues to the far corner office. The placard on the door reads *Sheriff Robert Durham*. He knocks three times and waits for a response.

From behind the door, a deep voice invites him in. The room is dark save for the natural light seeping in below the curtains.

On the walls are various accolades and certificates, side by side with watercolour paintings of famous football catches and signed prints of iconic photographs from other professional sports. On the desk is a taxidermied mallard, the green hues of its tail feathers accentuated by a ray of sunlight, and beside it a portrait of Sheriff Durham's family.

The sheriff himself has coiffed dark hair streaked with grey and white. His stubble is neat, groomed to the lines of his robust jaw.

All day he burns small cones of incense made from pressed sawdust from the mill just south of town. He stands one now on a small ceramic base, holds a lighter to the top of the cone until it glows orange, and then places overtop of it a tiny model log cabin made from the same ceramic as the base. The smoke billows from its minuscule chimney as if a family of insect-sized people were trying to keep warm indoors. The entire room smells like a wood-burning stove.

Arnason, you pussy willow. What can I do you for? Durham asks.

We've got a kid in room four right now.

Great, he says. He throws his hands in the air as if to ask, *so what?*

Yeah, Arnason says. He hesitates. I don't know what to make of it.

You never were the sharpest knife in the drawer.

The kid in four says he killed somebody.

Is that right? Who'd he kill?

He says he's the one that did our dead carnie.

At this bit of information, the sheriff sits straight up. His entire body seems to stiffen at the suggestion. I was told that boy fell.

That's what we thought, too. But this kid is in here now and he's saying otherwise. He's saying they were in an argument and he pushed him.

He's saying it was an accident?

Look, he's nervous as all hell, Bob, sweating and pale green in the face. I don't think he's lying.

The sheriff takes a round black tin from his top drawer, removes the lid, and packs a pinch of long, straight-cut tobacco into a ball. He tucks it behind his front lip. Arnason can see him working the dip around in the small pocket of his gums below his front teeth.

You know what you're going to tell him, don't you, Deputy?

What am I gonna tell him? Arnason can tell Durham is poking at the dip with the tip of his tongue and it makes his stomach turn over.

You're going to tell him what I read right here at my desk this morning in that report from Martens. That boy fell.

I don't think this kid is going to accept that from me. He's dead-set, Bob. You can see it in his face.

You're gonna tell him he's confused. Sheriff Durham takes the white coffee cup from his desk, pulls it up to his lips, and spits. He's mistaken.

DALLAN DERMOTT

There is something about having uttered it, said it out loud in a small room with no one else but the man with the horse tie to hear him, that makes Dallan's shoulders settle. What he did— it can't be undone. But the official nature of his confession has absolved him of some of what he feared to be insurmountable guilt. His cheeks flush with blood and his forehead grows warm, the colour returning to his face.

He takes a sip from the glass of water set out before him on the metal table. He waits for what feels like no time at all before the door to the room opens again. The same man with dark eyes enters the room and reassumes his position in the seat opposite of Dallan.

So, he says. This kid you say you killed, do you know his name?

No, sir.

And you say nobody saw what you think happened?

That's right. He says this, but thinks again of the girl, of Hannah.

Do you know anything about this kid?

Nothing, sir.

The man sits back and almost seems to relax for a moment. Nobody else does, either, he says.

Dallan is silent, caught off guard.

Nobody knows anything about the victim. His boss with the Carlsbad outfit has his name and not much else. We've recorded it here as an accident officially, that he likely fell while performing some routine maintenance in the back there behind the Ferris wheel.

But I told you—I'm telling you it wasn't like that.

We've got a statement from a credible witness on our records that indicates it was, in fact, like that.

I'm telling you the truth.

I don't think you are. I think you're lying to me. And lying to the police is a bookable offence.

I don't know what I have to say to make you believe me. Dallan's voice is shrill and desperate.

You're lying, kid. I don't know why the hell you are, but if you don't shut your mouth and get out of this police station I'll put you in a fucking cell. You're going to have real trouble. Are you hearing me?

Dallan stares back at the man, eyes narrowed. He feels his anger bulge in his throat.

That's as far as we're going to take this. The man drums his fingers on the tabletop, stiff gaze fixed right back on Dallan. It's going to stay that way on paper.

The eye contact is too much for Dallan and he shifts his attention to the two-way mirror occupying the half-wall behind the officer.

There's nobody in there, the officer says. His voice has softened. It's just you and me here. That kid you say you pushed—accidentally, I'll add—he doesn't have a person in the world. You, I'm assuming, have your parents in town. You probably have friends, other family, maybe a nice girl waiting for you some place around here. You probably have a decent job. Maybe you're thinking about college. Maybe you're already there.

Dallan is slow to process. What he's said is the truth. His eyes begin to wander around the room, desperate for someone to validate his disbelief.

The officer slams a hand down onto the table to regain his attention.

Listen. You're going to walk out of here and you're going to go home. Hell, go back to the Sunsetter grounds and have a beer with your buds. Have a smoke. I don't care. But you're going to forget about this false account bullshit.

I don't understand, Dallan says.

Get it through your head. We've got enough on our plates around here. Another kid, a young man from Perron, this town right here—he died last night, too. Looks like an overdose. The locals, the papers, they're going to be on our asses looking for answers when that gets out.

Brooks. Of course they know about him. He watched as those other officers held the perimeter around the paramedics. Dallan imagines he should feel relieved at this revelation, but instead his anger blooms.

That's what we care about here, the officer says. Not some poor transient fuck who probably would have kicked it in the next city over, or the one after that, scrawny little shit stain getting off on picking fights.

What the man is saying goes against everything Dallan has ever known about actions having consequences, about people being held accountable in the world. Something in his face must have telegraphed this to the officer, who slaps the table one more time with his closed fist. Hey. Look at me. He points a finger at Dallan. This station will rain the very fire of hell on you if you don't keep your mouth shut. You hear me?

Dallan looks him right in the eyes and he says, Yes, sir.

Without another word, the officer stands, sending his folding metal chair falling backwards to the ground, and leaves Dallan alone once more.

DEPUTY ARNASON

He cups his hands beneath the faucet and fills them with cool water, takes a sip, slurping through his pursed lips, and then splashes another handful over his face. With a finger plugging one side and then the other, he blows his nose into the sink and rinses himself away from the white enamel basin.

In the mirror, he opens his eyes as wide as he can. They are yellowed around the irises. Small jagged dashes of red peek out from beneath the edges of his eyelids and below them are the dark bags that have grown deeper in colour, heavier in recent years. His conversation with that kid has aged him another ten, he thinks. He can see it all over his face.

The door to the washroom swings open behind him and Durham comes in. His steps echo in the otherwise empty tiled room. He goes straight for the line of urinals on the wall opposite the sink. He stands stiff, legs spread. Arnason can hear him undo the fly of his pants and then the urine against the hard porcelain.

So? Durham says. He speaks into the empty advertisement slot on the wall above the urinal.

Arnason tears a piece of paper towel from the dispenser and wipes his face. So what?

What happened with the kid?

We sent him off maybe ten minutes ago. I did what you said.

Did you scare him?

He was rattled, sure.

Good, Durham says. He arches his back as one last burst of liquid hits the urinal. Then he zips his fly and buckles his belt. At the sink, he stands beside Arnason and rinses his hands. Fear is a tool and we've got it ready at the hip. He taps his service weapon in its holster. We're practically fucking dripping with it. Look at us, Arnason. Who's better than us?

Arnason looks at himself in the mirror and then at the man at his side, his boss in both his professions, legitimate and otherwise. Both of them are wearing their standard issue pleated khakis, their unassuming collared shirts and traditional rodeo weekend novelty ties, badges fastened at their waists.

Durham shakes the water off his hands and bares his teeth in the mirror, checking them for chewing tobacco. They are yellowed, darker along the tight spaces between them. That Xerox on the fritz again? Durham asks.

Always is.

Tell that mouth breather Martens that I want him to go up the street and make me copies of all the reports from last night. I caught him sleeping in his cruiser last night when he was supposed to be on patrol. And get changed, Durham says. We're going for a drive.

†

There are only three vehicles in evidence lock-up. It's rare that a car gets seized in town, though sometimes the impound guys will bring a stray around if they think there's something fishy about the way it looks, where it was parked and for how long. Right now, they've got the choice between a low-riding Honda with a spoiler they took off some kid for drag racing in the industrial park and two pickups that have seen better days.

Better go with one of the trucks, Durham says. That hotrod is too conspicuous.

I know for a fact the green one has a busted head gasket, Arnason says. It'll overheat on the highway. Let's take the Ford.

Durham drives. They take Donahue Street out of downtown. The once vibrant window displays of boutiques and bakeries have been replaced with insurance agencies and smoke shops, or else have remained vacant ever since the oil money left Perron. They merge onto the highway heading north. They're quiet in the way they usually are together on their rides, Durham pointing out his favourite cups of truck stop coffee or the exits to the reservations where he buys his chew in bulk. A semi-truck passes them, a plush purple rabbit zap-strapped to the front grill, its faux fur matted with mud and oil.

They continue past the awkward brush interrupted by irrigation ditches and stubble fields. The closer they get to the lab, the denser the stands of trees are along the sides of the highway, the trunks of the dark blue-green conifers huddled close amongst deadfall and saplings.

Deputy, Durham says. We've got to talk. Mano-a-mano.

The Sheriff only ever calls Arnason by his rank when he's about to cut him down. The last time was after Arnason was seen by some straight cops handing off a resupply to one of his dealers in town. When they came to Durham to report the suspicious activity, the sheriff called Arnason in to defend himself in front of the accusers, right there on the spot, totally unprepared. Arnason came up with some bullshit about delivering clandestine intel to a couple of sources in the local skinhead scene. If the two cops knew any better, the entire thing would have sounded as ridiculous and improbable as it truly was in Perron, but they had been with the precinct for less than a year and still had highly imaginative hunches about an organized crime network operating in the seedy underbelly of their rural county along with pipe dreams of busting it up.

Durham's operation with the folks up north is as close as anything gets to big city crime around here, and since Arnason has been involved, it's been a single product retail operation. Not that they wouldn't all be going away for a very long time if any of it ever came out.

Sure, Arnason answers. Straight talk.

Doing what we do, you know we always need contingency plans. We need to have our shit in order in case things go south.

Of course.

You've been my go-to for a while now. You're trustworthy, loyal. I'd call you my right-hand man.

I appreciate that.

And in this business, sometimes we need an individual to play the hero, to be a sacrificial lamb. I'm not saying we need anyone like that right now, right this instant, but we're in deep, both of us and the other guys, too, and if anything goes wrong we need to protect the majority.

Arnason is seldom surprised by anything Durham says. He's a man of empty platitudes and predictability and this current speech hasn't exactly caught him off guard, either, though the line of thinking, the direction Durham is taking, has resentment simmering in Arnason. In truth, he knows what's coming and has known for some time.

I'll put it to you straight, Arnason. If it ever comes out that our department has its hands in this pill pushing shit, we have to point the finger at someone—or everyone goes down.

Out of curiosity, sir.

Deputy.

Why not you?

With all due respect, Arnason, I brought you in. I brought you all in. You've all sucked at the teat and now you're fat and happy. And so am I. But hell if I'm going down for making you all a bunch of money. We need to make it look like one bad egg, one rogue officer. It needs to be someone senior enough. It's gotta make sense.

And that's me?

It's you. Our associates have already agreed on it. It's done. I'm telling you as a courtesy. I'm doing you a solid. It could be all this goes down one day and you come into work and—surprise, bitch—find everyone pointing the finger at you. No. That's not the way I like to do things. If shit goes sour, you'll know ahead of time and you'll be well prepared. Those on the inside will testify against you, and the ones who know nothing will say exactly that. Nothing.

Arnason clenches his molars. His feet cramp at their arches inside his boots. And what if I decline? he says. Respectfully, of course, sir.

Sheriff Durham punches his fist into the centre of the wheel. The truck horn bellows. Arnason jumps in his seat.

There'll be no fucking negotiation, Durham says. This is not a discussion. This is a goddamn order.

Arnason's eyes are glued on the road ahead, but in his mind he sees nothing but white hot indignation. He's been reliable for Durham. He's always there to smooth things over or take care of the dirty work, but for a long time now he's sensed the possibility of their operation's demise. The manufacturers up north have amped up supply and, in turn, Durham has grown bold and callous in the way he conducts business, taking on new dealers through nothing more than word of mouth, authorizing sales to the kids in the middle schools with their wispy upper lips and hairless pits. Arnason knows cutting corners is a fast way to get fucked in this business, but he's kept his mouth shut. He's been a good soldier and now it looks like he's expected to go out like one, too. Still, he keeps quiet. He prides himself on knowing when to keep quiet.

They turn off at a range road where a billboard advertises a motel nearby with jacuzzi tubs and continental breakfast. On the left is a field of barley seedlings enclosed in a short barbed wire fence. A different mesh-back hat is nailed to the top of each pole. On the right is more of the same dense wood. Another fifteen minutes and they're surrounded again on both sides by spruce and pine.

Durham pulls off onto a nondescript turnoff and idles the truck. There is a rusted farm gate blocking the narrow dirt road that leads into the forest. Durham steps down from the cab, removes a ring of keys from his pocket, and opens the padlock.

The branches of the trees that flank the haggard road hang low and brush against the windshield and side windows as they drive slowly down the dim path. There are no markers on the shoulders, no signs of habitation. The ground rolls with ruts and potholes, a product of spring thaw and the preceding rains, hardened now with the recent dry heat uncharacteristic of May. Arnason sways in his seat. His head knocks against the plastic handle fastened to the roof on the passenger side.

They come to a fork, one path going out into a pasture and the other heading back off into the treeline. Durham goes left, further into the woods. The old growth canopy above them is so thick that the daylight shines down on them in a filtered semi-glow. Rays manage to sneak through in clear bands and illuminate dust and debris like blinking satellites in the obscurity ahead. It reminds Arnason of the spaceships in the movies, when they punch into warp speed and the stars that punctuate the vacuum of black space ahead stretch and elongate in the camera's periphery.

At the end of the road is a tall chain-link gate crowned with stainless concertina wire. Durham once again gets out to unlock it. Up ahead about a dozen feet, Arnason can see the tree branches part to the open sky. They drive on into a clearing of hardened dirt marked by tire tracks, fenced in on every side. A group of muddy vehicles is parked along the far treeline with a couple ATVs and big-wheeled dirt bikes. As they approach, two men stare them down from the wooden porch of a double-wide trailer.

No talking, Durham says. He shuts off the engine.

Why are we out here again?

They asked for a face-to-face, Durham says. It's about those two kids from last night.

Arnason cracks his neck. His stomach sinks. After this, he doesn't want to hear another word about those boys.

They walk past the double-wide and Arnason nods his head at the two men, each with a steaming enamel mug of coffee between their hands. One of them wears a waterproof Gore-Tex shell while the other has a waxed canvas overcoat on. These men up here, they've always looked a little too high-brow for Arnason's preconception of drug manufacturers, with their high-priced out-erwear and well-oiled beards.

Past the trailer is a large garden with the first sprouts of the season rising from the soil like wisps of frozen green vapour. Further still is a massive hangar-like structure constructed from sheet metal, spray-painted a deep green like the conifers. There are pallets stacked along the wall as well as crates, both wooden and aluminum, blue plastic barrels, and dark metal drums littering the yard around the warehouse.

They approach the hangar door and Durham knocks twice against the siding, each blow reverberating through the entire wall and echoing within. The door slides open and a man in a short winter hat rolled just above his ears shakes their hands and beckons them inside.

They're led through the centre of the vast hangar. A sharp chemical smell tingles Arnason's nose. On one side is a row of stainless steel stills, each seven or eight feet high, connected to each other through a series of pipes and chutes. On the otherside are several steel-top shop tables, individuals seated on tall stools working away under the direct light of medical lamps, and behind them against the wall are more blue plastic barrels, some so worn from travel and use that they appear almost black.

The warehouse is lit by huge halogen floodlights hanging from the roof. At the very far end is a small office and the yellow incandescence from its windows stands out in an environment otherwise bathed in white. The man who guides them opens the door and steps aside. Durham enters first and Arnason follows.

The room is furnished in the utilitarian aesthetic of a medical facility, stainless steel desks and working surfaces with rolling chairs and more high stools to match. The floor is spotless white linoleum and the walls are decorated with carefully placed maps and new wave concert posters, like the secret basecamp of fashionable teenagers planning a guerilla rebellion.

A man in a black quilted vest, elastic cuffed pants, and tall hiking boots turns away from one of the maps on the far wall to greet them.

What's good, friends? I'm so glad you could make the drive.

Anytime, Durham says. He opens his arms to him like he is seeing a family member or an old friend.

Was it okay getting here?

Took a minute.

I know we're kind of tucked away out here, but you've got to admit, the natural setting is gorgeous.

Lush, Arnason says.

Have a seat and let's chat.

Arnason and Durham sit in the two office chairs in front of the main desk. The surface is bare save for a closed white laptop and a USB extension port with various charging cords attached.

We've heard there was an incident—two incidents—at your big event last night.

Durham nods.

Tell me. What happened?

Durham looks to Arnason. He shoots him a look back. He told him not to talk. But after an awkward silence, he takes over.

We had one kid kick it not too late into the night, Arnason says. The paramedics called it an OD. The other one, we're not too concerned about. Hit his head. An accident.

You're not concerned?

We've got a witness statement confirming he fell, Durham says.

The man spins a black pen around the knuckle of his index finger. I understand this individual was working for you?

Not directly.

But indirectly?

He was pushing for our buyer in the carnival company.

I see. He stops spinning the pen and places it on the desk. How well do you know this contact?

We've had an arrangement since our first year working with you, Durham says. He's solid. Real meticulous. And he's a big fish, a very generous customer.

So the dealer then, did he have anything on him?

We took care of that, Arnason says.

Alright. I trust you both out there. You're the ones we would need to be worried about doing any sniffing around, isn't that right? The man takes an impeccably rolled joint from the desk and lights it. But here you are, he says.

We've got it covered, Durham says.

The man holds the joint out to Durham, then Arnason. He waves his hand to decline.

Arnason cuts in again. About this overdose.

Durham kicks Arnason in the boot.

The man draws at the joint and the cherry glows. He fills his chest and exhales blue smoke simultaneously from his mouth and nose. Yes, he says, wisps still streaming from between his lips. Go on.

Arnason shoots Durham a flat look. Then he goes on. It's just, we haven't seen anything like this happen before. Not with the pills. Kids are taking this shit all the time and it just doesn't happen.

You're right. It hasn't happened. But I think I can explain.

By all means, then, Arnason says. He waves his hand in a circle like an old-fashioned gentleman.

We've been cutting batches with trace amounts of fentanyl. I'm talking about microscopic amounts, so small you could hardly even see it with the naked eye. It's cheap, easy to get our hands on, and it enhances the experience for our customers. We can use less of the expensive shit and sell it for even more. High is high, right?

Obviously not, Arnason says. We've got a dead kid on our hands and come Monday morning people are going to want answers.

We're very careful. This is pretty exact chemistry—I won't confuse you two with the technical details. But I'll say it's possible, due to some kind of human error, that a dose or two may have been overdone.

Human error?

Manual mistake. You know, a shaky hand? A generous pour?

Arnason shakes his head and leans in over the desk. A generous fucking pour? he says.

Hold on, Durham says. He places a firm hand on Arnason's shoulder, guides him to the back of his chair. Look, we can't have this. No more dead kids. Especially not this weekend.

We're aware of how important this whole redneck brouhaha of yours is for business. We don't want to scare off any potential customers.

If anything else newsworthy happens, this'll all come tumbling down for everyone. The shit storm will be upon us.

The man appears calm, indifferent. It won't happen again, he says.

Good, Durham says.

In fact, we've resupplied you with a fresh batch to make sure this is nothing more than an isolated incident. A blip. He snaps his fingers.

We'll take it back with us then, says Durham.

It's already been shipped. It's waiting for you in the usual spot. The man picks up what remains of his joint with a pair of tweezers and takes a long pull at the roach. He smiles at Durham and Arnason, smoke seeping out of his mouth and into his nose in a toothy French inhale.

HANNAH FIELDS

W hen her tears finally ran out the night before, her eyes swollen and red, she closed them and slept an unusual sleep, one that did not break for the dream world or the waking one for a full eight hours until the sound of her mother's vacuum in the hallway finally jostled her awake.

There was no grace period, no foggy headspace between sleeping and waking in which she was able to forget for even a moment what had happened to Nick. The truth of it had been like a sad and loyal dog waiting at the door of her mind for her to return to consciousness. When she did, it numbed her inside and out.

All morning, this reality follows her from her bed to the bathroom to her bed again. She pictures Nick there in the dirt, cast in the blue light of the Ferris wheel. She can't remember the last words they spoke out loud to each other. She could check her phone for their final text messages, but even those are from over a week ago now, and what was a text message to her anyway? In her mind, she could try to read them in his voice, imagine him speaking the awkward shorthand and abbreviated *I love yous*, but that only formed a figment, an approximation of the person that he was. She is tired of imagining him. She has been doing that for over a year and it occurs to her that she knows this version of Nick, the person she has dreamed up and cobbled together from pictures and words and grainy phone calls from far and remote places, better than the person she met at the Sunsetter last May. The entire time it all felt so real to her, but now it might as well have been a juvenile fantasy.

There is a knock at her door, but she doesn't answer. Another knock, and then it opens.

Her mother stands in the doorway and cocks her head. She knows nothing of the events of the previous night, that her daughter is so tucked away inside herself it's like she is underwater.

Breakfast is waiting, her mother says.

Hannah moves the covers from over the bottom half of her face. I'm not hungry, she says, muffled by the blanket.

Cowboy breakfast. The rodeo weekend classic. I made it for you.

I'm not hungry.

Would you just come down for a little bit?

Why?

It's early afternoon. It's a beautiful day.

Hannah thinks she might like to see the sun, that maybe if she stares straight at it for long enough it might sear all memory and emotion from her brain. She pushes the covers off her body with her feet, kick by kick, knowing if she thinks too long about the task it will become impossible, and rises to follow her mother.

The sun is underwhelming. The same feeling of inexpressible loss joins her at the kitchen table. She refuses to eat. After her mother finally clears away the plate full of scrambled eggs, quick-fry steak, black beans, and toast, Hannah spreads out her newest paint-by-numbers canvas before her on the table with a tray of acrylics ready for her brush. This particular piece is from Monet's famous series of water lilies, the ones from his own flower garden in Giverny. She works to recreate the soft palate and swirling strokes of his brush, the hazy quality she imagines was a product of the cataracts that made his eyes ghost-like and milky white later in his life.

She wishes for lilies like these to sprout up from the small inflatable pool in her own backyard, the one that her family dog, Scobey, used to wade in to keep himself cool in the summer, surrounded by patches of grass yellowed by his urine. This was the last thing she remembers him enjoying before he passed away from old age the month before.

She wets her brush in a white mug of clear water and begins mixing the greens and yellows in search of the perfect earthly balance. When she thinks she's found it, she applies the paint lightly with her brush to all the spaces marked with the number thirteen.

She continues on like this, mixing and dabbing and painting, until Nick is only a small flicker in the back of her mind, like a bulb whose filament is about to give out. She has always dealt with hardship this way, concentrating on the hundreds of tiny fragments, an unfinished mosaic seeking to deconstruct the complexity of a nuanced piece of art.

Scobey had taken his post at her feet all the long days and nights of the past year when she refused to go out with friends and instead stayed at home in her bed talking on the phone with Nick or messaging him. Over time, she'd come to associate the dog with Nick and that made it that much harder when Scobey passed. She completed twelve other Monets during the month she grieved him. Scobey was first and now it's Nick and it occurs to her that maybe this time painting will not be enough. The small flashes of his absence refuse to give way to the exhaustive task laid out before her.

There is a knock at the front door, down the hall from the kitchen. Her parents have gone now, running errands or visiting family like they normally do on the weekends, maybe even taking in some of the events at the Sunsetter grandstand. She places her brush in the cup. The paint that lingers between the bristles disperses in the water like the bottom of a clear lake kicked up by a swimmer's feet.

She goes to the front entrance, expects a neighbour calling on her parents or else some door-to-door salesman or solicitor. But when she turns the deadbolt and opens up the door, it's the boy from school, the one from the night before.

Her mind is overwhelmed by images of Nick, his colourless face, of this boy at her door standing over him. She wants to slam it shut. His presence is a vise being wrenched around her chest. His eyes give him away, though, a desperate pain in them. It's as if they are begging her to see him, to hear him out. She holds the door halfway open.

He is, at first, slow to speak. His mouth hangs open only a touch, like he has something he wants to say but has lost it somewhere between the place he has just come from and her front doorstep. For a moment, they stand there on either side of the door's threshold, taking each other in.

He speaks first. He says her name. Hannah.

She lowers her eyes, but then responds in the way she almost always does when answering the door. Yes, she says. How are you?

Sorry?

I mean, what can I do for you? She shakes her head. What do you want?

I need to talk to you, he says. But only if you want to talk to me.

There is something small about him, a fragility or warped weakness, and she can't tell if she should feel contempt or pity for him.

We're talking now, aren't we? she says. I guess I don't really have a choice at this point.

I can leave, he says.

She considers shutting the door right there in his face, but she also remembers the promise he made the night before, that he would turn himself in first thing in the morning. She wants to remind him of that promise—he can't have made good on it yet if he's still free and walking around town. Go around the back, she says. I'll meet you in the yard.

She locks up again and goes to the sliding door at the opposite end of the house. Outside, she takes two folding chairs, the kind with the colourful vinyl thread weaved together into crisscrossed bands strung over a hollow aluminum frame. The chairs have faded and frayed from years left out in inclement weather. She brings them over to the edge of the small inflatable pool and gestures for Dallan to take a seat. At the spigot to the right of the patio door, she runs the water and then drags the green rubber hose along the grass to the pool. She begins to fill it. When it is ankle deep, she shuts the water off and returns to take a seat beside Dallan, the metal of the chair's frame hot from the sun against her calves. She pulls off her white socks and places her feet in the shallow pool.

Well, she says to Dallan.

I went to the police station. I turned myself in.

Then how are you here in my backyard?

Dallan raises his head, seems to have missed the absurdity in his previous statement given the circumstances. I mean, I tried to turn myself in.

You *tried*?

Exactly. He takes a deep breath. He tells her about the interrogation room and the officer with the dark eyes and cowboy tie and the initial cursory questions. Then he left for a couple minutes, and when he came back he just told me I was free to go. He winces at this next part. Your friend, the guy who worked at Sunsetter, the officer told me nobody cared about him. Like he was just a stranger to everybody, someone who didn't matter.

This hurts her. It isn't true.

He pauses for her response but she gives him none. Then he says, He asked me if anybody saw it happen.

Hannah is quiet and attentive. It's as if she is watching the conversation happen on a television screen, in a reality beyond her own. Her own head is a quiet place for the scenes to rest untouched until they disappear from her consciousness, replaced by some other combination of light and sound and other sensation.

She blinks hard to regain focus. What did you tell him? she asks.

I told him, no.

And that's it?

They said they had a witness statement. Someone told them that it was an accident, that he fell. Did you talk to the cops?

You told me to get help.

You could have said you found him there.

I was trying to help *you*.

Now that they have your statement, that's as far as they're going to take it. That's what they told me.

She is shaking her head, over and over. So you just left? Why didn't you *make* him hear you out?

Dallan is flustered. His hands fumble and roll over one another. He scratches at the coarse threading on the seams of his pants. You don't understand. He reaches down to the pool and splashes a bit of water on his wrists. Something wasn't right about it. He wouldn't hear me. He wouldn't listen.

Nick wasn't nobody. He had his family back east. Then she pauses. He was going to stay here. He had me.

When Dallan doesn't answer, she looks up from the rippling pool and sees him beside her in all his helplessness.

And what about your friend? she asks him.

Brooks. He winces as he says it.

Brooks, she says. Did the police say anything about him?

They said he's the dead person they care about. It was like they thought—Dallan swallows. Nick. It was like they thought he'd be a distraction. But more than that. Like dealing with him would be a problem for them.

Her eyes sting but can't muster any more tears from her ducts. Why don't we just go to the paper or the news or something? We can post it online, send it to anyone who might care. We can tell them what really happened.

You don't get it, Dallan says. That cop, he said it would be bad if I mouthed off about this to anyone. Like, really bad. Scary bad. He looked dead serious.

She grinds her teeth. It still doesn't make sense to her. Leave, she tells him. She points to the walkway. Get out.

Dallan is taken aback.

Get the fuck out of here, she shouts.

His chest raises as if he is about to speak, but then he sinks back into himself. He lets the air out from his chest. He gets up and leaves.

When he is gone, she notices her hands are tight around the white plastic armrests of the lawn chair. Her entire body is clenched and the skin of her cheeks is clamped between her molars. Her throat is hoarse. What right did he have to walk away from the Sunsetter last night, or that police station this morning? What right did he have to walk away from all of this so freely?

Then her grip loosens and each muscle group follows suit. Despite the grief that has been numbing her mind, making everything feel distant and indistinguishable, she remembers the remorse in his face when she first opened the door. She believes he did not mean to hurt Nick, and that if he could, he would take back what happened the night before. She believes he tried sincerely to do the right thing and turn himself in this morning, but what he says happened after, what went down between him and the police, she can't make sense of.

What occurred last night is still fresh in her mind and body. But it is also irrevocably in the past, an absence of sound after a wind has passed and all the leaves in the forest have come back to stasis. She knows that the past is not a place she wants to dwell in. It is too quiet, too bleak.

She takes her feet out of the pool. She feels the blades of grass bend without breaking beneath the softness of her bare feet as she comes around the house. Out front, she finds Dallan still standing at the foot of the driveway, staring out into the street. She calls to him and he turns.

You said something last night, she says. That Nick sold you guys something and that's how Brooks died?

Dallan nods and swallows. He tells her how Brooks knew Nick would be selling and from which tent, about the kid from the rodeo crew going around the high school tipping people off. He tells her about the system with the money and the stick of gum, about the bush party and the walk back to the midway after they took the pills. He describes the paramedics and the crowd and how Brooks's lips had gone purple, his hands cold.

Nick's not coming back. I know that, she says. But I knew him and he wouldn't ever hurt anyone. Not on purpose.

Maybe this can be her distraction, her solution to grief. Maybe if she works with Dallan, she can piece together the disappearance of the life she desperately wanted, the one she nearly had.

†

Thomas is Hannah's brother. He lives in a second storey walk-up apartment called the Amber Arms south of downtown. Buildings like his used to house the oil field and construction workers when they first came to Perron from all over the country, even places the world over that most people in Perron had probably never heard of. Now they're cheap rentals for young locals or the now-unemployed who never left. The building's stucco has been weather-stained to a drab grey colour. Dark streaks run down the walls where the water overflows from the eavestroughs crammed with years of decomposing leaves and other detritus. Hannah parks her mother's impeccable sedan in one of the guest spots and leads Dallan up the stairs.

When Thomas opens the door, he appears to have only just woken up. His eyes are red and his hair is sticking up awkwardly on the top of his head. He wears a pair of green sweatpants and a wrinkled white t-shirt with a faded brown stain streaking down the front. A musty, stale smell wafts out of the apartment and dilutes in the fresh air.

Sister, he says.

Hi, Thomas.

I haven't seen you in—shit—how long?

Months probably.

Probably.

I need to talk, she says.

Who's your friend?

He's from school, she says. Are you going to let us in?

It's not clean.

Is it ever?

What's this kid's name? he asks. He eyes Hannah's companion suspiciously.

Dallan Dermott, Hannah tells him.

Thomas looks back over his shoulder into the apartment, still obscured by the half-opened door. He sniffles a little and wipes his upper lip with the back of his hand. Then he beckons them inside.

The apartment is as promised. The shag carpet is pock-marked with dark spills and smaller burn spots from errant joints or cigarettes. There is a big screen television on one side of the room and on the other is a turquoise couch beneath a wrinkled poster of a generic cityscape, New York or London or maybe Berlin, she can't tell. Apart from the couch and the television and a teak coffee table in the middle of the room between them, there isn't much furniture and the walls are bare and scuffed in impossible places.

Thomas walks ahead and gathers trash from the coffee table. He stuffs foil takeout containers and three empty tall cans of beer into a brown paper takeout bag.

Take a seat, he says.

93

Dallan and Hannah sit on opposite ends of the couch while Thomas brings the garbage to the kitchen. Hannah eyes the semi-translucent leopard print bong beside the TV, full of murky water, glass stained ashen around the top lip. She watches her brother root around in the fridge.

Want anything to drink? he calls from the kitchen. I've got Red Bull.

Hannah answers him, says they're fine.

I could use a Red Bull, Dallan whispers.

Hannah shakes her head at him.

Thomas returns and from the pocket of his sweats he removes a can of beer and sits down in the centre of the couch between Hannah and Dallan. Last one. He shrugs and cracks the beer, grabs the remote from the table, and turns on the television, turning it down so the proceedings of a daytime courtroom show are barely audible.

This is unexpected, Thomas says.

I don't see you. You don't see me. It's fine, Hannah says. Were you sleeping?

Just kind of rolling around in bed.

Dallan is stiff as a mannequin, save for the subtle shaking of his hands as they move about over the surface of the pants on his thighs.

But seriously, Thomas says. You hardly ever visit and now you come rolling in on the morning of Sunsetter Saturday?

It's one in the afternoon, Hannah says.

It's morning for some of us around here, he says. This weekend, especially.

We wanted to ask you about something, Hannah says. She looks past her brother at Dallan. His shy nature is evident in Thomas's presence. He is lock-lipped, looking around the room nervously. We want to roll tonight, she says. But we have a few questions. Dallan does, mostly. He's nervous about it.

No fucking kidding, Thomas says. He evaluates Dallan. You wigging out, buddy?

Hannah is afraid her brother will go too hard on Dallan, that he'll make things even more tense and awkward than they already are. Thomas has always let her down. When they were younger, he joked around or mocked her when she needed him to be sincere, then told her off or sent her away when she sought out the kind of honest conversation possible between siblings. He has known her longer than anyone, how she's grown and changed over time. The previous spring when she met Nick, her brother was the only person she tried to tell, but he brushed her off, going on about how he didn't want to hear about his sister getting around. She never brought it up again. It's his friends he has always prioritized, the parties and the drugs and the drinking he has always chosen.

Now, again, she needs him. It's his world that holds the answers she's looking for, his expertise she needs.

Before we do it, Dallan wants to know where the stuff comes from, she says. Who makes it or whatever, what's in it. I thought you'd be the person to ask.

Thomas takes a long draught of his beer. If that was readily available information, don't you think we'd be hearing about it on the news or some shit?

Just tell us whatever you know and we'll leave you alone, Hannah says. I really want to do it tonight. Sunsetter Saturday, right? But he's the only one I'll do it with and he's bugging out on me.

Why him? Thomas asks. Are you two, like, together?

No, Dallan says. God no.

We're just friends, Hannah says. We had Home Ec together, back in junior year. We kind of hit it off, kept in touch, you know?

Why don't you roll with me tonight? Thomas says. I'm your brother. You trust this string bean more than you trust me?

Jesus Christ, Thomas. Just tell us or don't. Sometimes I can't fucking stand you.

Thomas seems to straighten out in response to her outburst. And why would I know anything about it anyway? he says.

So she builds him up. Rebellion has always been a source of pride for him and he wears his devil-may-care attitude on his sleeve around her and their parents. In high school, he stole their father's truck. Stoned and drunk, he crashed it through the window of a convenience store. He spent some time in juvenile detention for that. Not long after returning home, he got kicked out for stealing their mother's credit card to order cannabis seeds online and for the five years since he's been living in the same apartment, a five-minute drive from his family with hardly a visit from either side. He couldn't even keep the pot plants alive.

You're the only one I'd trust about this, she says.

Then I need you to do me a favour first.

And what's that?

I need you to swipe me grandpa's six shooter from the house.

She laughs. No way.

No deal, then.

I'm not stealing you a gun, Thomas.

I just want to do some target practice, that's all.

Go get a licence and buy one then.

He scoffs. Come on. No one taught me to shoot. Only you.

It's true. Hunting and shooting were critical to the Fields' idea of strength and independence—one that, in retrospect, seemed to apply to Hannah but not her brother. She hunted with her father and grandfather when she was young and both of them made sure she did her part. They hunted ducks on the wetlands to the northeast and white tail deer in November on the forested acres of their family farm. Thomas never came along. He showed little interest and her father always said he didn't have the temperament.

Just for her, their father would line metal targets along the shelterbelt of spruce trees. Each of them had a small arm with a circular target at the end. One side was painted blue, and if you hit a target it would spin around on a hinge and show red. She spent hours with her grandfather's pistol, firing shots at those tiny targets, loving the ping of the bullet striking the metal and the kickback of a firearm that did not rest against your shoulder but was rather held suspended in the air in front of you with only your own strength and balance to brace its force. She learned to crave the satisfaction of a row of red circles staring back at her from beneath the low branches of the spruce trees.

Fine, she says. Next weekend, I'll take you. But when we're done, the gun goes straight back in the case. No sketchiness.

Thomas can't help but smile a little. He nods.

So about the stuff? she says.

He leans back into the couch, throws his arms over his shoulders and lets them sink into the loose, worn-out cushioning. As far as what's in it, he says, most people have tester kits for that. You've gotta be smart about it with all the nasty shit out there. He pulls out a nylon pencil case from the sliding drawer of the coffee table and hands it to her. There might be instructions or something inside.

She takes it and unzips it. There are some small, medicinal-looking vials, a few empty pill bottles, an eye dropper, and a piece of folded paper.

The stuff here in Perron is almost always clean, though. In fact, the joke around here is that it has to be to even make it to the streets at all. The guys who distribute run a tight ship. They don't want too much attention.

Hannah looks at Dallan again and he rubs his thighs with the heels of his palms. Where does it come from? Like, South America or Asia or something?

Fuck no, he says. All domestic. There's a lab off the grid somewhere north of here, but anyone who knows exactly where is either working there or dead. Probably. Thomas laughs and puts his arm around his sister. I miss you. You should come around more often. Hell, I'd hook you up right now if I had any on me.

I guess that's my other question, Hannah says. Where can we find it?

At Sunsetter? he spits. You'll probably find a dozen tablets if you walk up and down the midway and keep your eyes on the ground. That shit is everywhere this weekend.

Yeah, yeah, she says. But who deals? We're not just going to swallow pills from the ground.

He stands, then paces around the room. His energy is noticeable discussing this. He relishes the chance to display his niche knowledge. Abruptly, he turns and points at her like a hunting dog signalling prey. You know what? I'm going down there tonight. Why don't the two of you come here and pre-drink with me and some buds? We'll all head to the grounds together and I'll get my guy to hook you up.

Sweet, Hannah says. That's perfect. She's almost lost track of where she first intended to go with the conversation. Thomas takes the remote from the coffee table and turns the volume on the television up ten bars and then down fifteen, up and down, up and down.

Dallan speaks up. Where does *he* get it? Your guy, I mean.

Thomas curls his top lip over the bottom and blows air down his chin. He'd never tell me, he says. People say nobody can protect you, not the cops or your own muscle. Nobody. Not if you fuck with the supply chain around here. Moreno used to deal here in Perron until they fucked him bad over some disagreement. That's the way he tells it, anyway. Now he flips patties at Burger Boss. Swears it's an upgrade.

Thomas hardly pays any attention to them as he speaks now, his eyes staring blankly at the television. He was made before, Moreno. Upgrade my ass. He plays air drums along with a song from a commercial, shifts and spins on the balls of his feet. He picks up his beer, tips it back, and crushes the aluminum can, empty, in his hand.

DEPUTY ARNASON

Back at the station, he settles in his office chair and watches Durham trudge across the room between the cubicles to his office. Arnason has a calendar pinned to his bulletin board, filled in with his mother's various medical appointments, due dates for monthly and weekly reports, personal reminders jotted down onto sticky notes in his wife's handwriting. He scans the month over, side to side, without registering the specifics of any of the notes.

He shares a cubicle with Martens and has for some time. Martens is hunched over his computer, a puzzle game open on his browser. He stares into his screen, so close his nose is nearly touching the monitor, with an attention reserved for only the most complicated tasks of the mind. He clicks on the various squares of the multicoloured grid and Arnason can hear the digital bass and spacey snare, the shrill auto-tuned vocals buzzing from his bulky headphones in the quiet of the near-empty office.

Shit for brains, Arnason says.

Martens does not turn around.

Hey, he says. Hey, fucker.

Martens is oblivious. Arnason scoots over in his rolling chair and kicks Martens's backrest.

Christ, Martens says. He rips the headphones from his ears. You scared the shit out of me.

What are you listening to?

EDM.

What the fuck is EDM?

Electronic dance music, Martens says. It helps me concentrate.

Arnason gestures to Marten's computer, the game on pause. Important work?

I'm taking a break. Breaks are crucial to productivity. Do you even *read*?

Arnason does a full spin in his office chair in the middle of the cubicle. Ever since his conversation with Durham on the way up north, he's been tense with nervous energy.

Martens goes to replace his headphones, but before he can, Arnason says, I went up north with Durham this morning.

Martens pauses with the headphones hovering over his ears. I know that, he says.

We grilled them pretty hard about our two dead kids.

Oh yeah? What'd they say about that OD?

They blamed it on manual error, Arnason says. Said it won't happen again.

Good, Martens says. That's the kind of shit that makes me want to drop everything and move to Venezuela. That kid, he was so, so—still? It wasn't natural.

So what? He was dead.

Death is natural, Martens says. I know. I get death. It happens to all of us. But not that way. We human beings were never meant to go out like that.

Arnason tugs at the hairs protruding ever so slightly out of his nostrils. He pulls one out and winces, feels the burn behind his eyes, and fights off a sneeze. Durham and I, he says, we had a conversation on our way up there.

Martens slumps in his chair. And what did you talk about?

Business. The future. A contingency plan.

Martens rolls his hand in the air, gestures at him to go on.

Basically, he told me that if our role in this ever gets out, I'm the guy who goes down. The fall guy.

Right, Martens says. I know that, too.

What do you mean you know that?

Durham told us last week.

He told you?

He took us all out for dinner last week. Remember? You had something going on with your mother or your wife. He took us out for tomahawk steaks at Georgie's and told us all that you were going to be the scapegoat if things went sideways, that we should all point the finger at you.

He told you that?

Yeah, and everyone else, too. He even had these brochures with exactly what we're supposed to say and everything. Told us to burn them after we'd committed them to memory.

Before he told me?

Martens shrugs. Look, I'm sorry. I thought you knew. I figured he filled you in before us.

Arnason curses Durham under his breath. He takes his ceramic coffee mug and smashes it against his desk, the cup separating from the handle and the leftover coffee splashing onto his hand and desk and keyboard.

Durham's door opens across the room. What the hell was that racket? he calls to them.

Martens looks at Arnason for the answer.

Arnason wipes the coffee from his hands onto his pants, the

white handle of the shattered mug still clenched in his other fist.

It was nothing, he says.

One more time? Durham calls.

Nothing, Arnason yells back.

DALLAN DERMOTT

They wait in line at Burger Boss, the first building in a long line of them—an antiques shop, an oil change franchise, a twenty-four-hour liquor store—all beside the highway on the north side of town. It's late for lunch, but eight or so patrons are queued up between the blue metal railings. One by one, customers approach the cashier and place their orders, then wander off to find a place to sit with their fountain drinks and plastic tabletop numbers.

When it's finally their turn, Dallan looks up at the backlit menu. Hannah walks to the counter first without looking back to see if he has followed. He shuffles up to join her.

We're looking for Moreno. Is he working today? she asks.

The teenager at the register appears barely awake, his eyelids half-shut. One sec, he says. I'll grab him. He goes over to the warming trays and ducks down so he can shout through the opening to the kitchen. He calls Moreno's name, says something else in a language other than English.

After thirty seconds or so, a short man with broad shoulders and a pronounced chest, mid-twenties, passes by the fryer and approaches them at the counter. What's up? he says.

These two asked for you.

Moreno looks them over. Yeah?

I'm Thomas's sister.

I see that, he says. You two look alike. How is Strawberry Fields?

She hasn't heard her brother's old high school nickname in years, a nod to his long strawberry blond hair, and she's hit with a pang of nostalgia. The same, she says.

Good, Moreno says. Good.

Dallan and Hannah stand there, wordless for a moment, the shiny blue counter between them reflecting the profiles of the cashier and Moreno.

So what do you want? he finally asks.

We were hoping to talk with you real quick, Hannah says. About your old job.

Moreno's brow furrows. Nah, he says. Not interested.

We're not looking for trouble, Hannah says.

You might not know it, he says. But you probably are.

We're on your side, Dallan says.

I don't have a side. I don't touch that anymore.

Just a few questions, Hannah says.

Totally anonymous, Dallan adds.

Moreno shakes his head. You're a good-looking girl, he says to Hannah, and me and your brother go way back. So I'm going to do you a solid. But not here. He turns to the cashier. I'm going for a smoke, okay? Be back in ten.

The cashier shrugs.

Meet me out back, Moreno says.

When they come around the building, Moreno is already leaning against the dumpster, lighting his cigarette. Dallan and Hannah stop at the edge of the garbage enclosure. Before either of them can say anything, Moreno raises his hands at them, waves them one over the other.

Look, he says. I don't sell anymore. My mom worked her ass off nannying to get us here from Manila and I nearly fucked that up. If you're looking to buy, I can't help you.

That's not why we're here, Hannah says.

Well, give it to me then. He blows a cloud of white smoke straight up into the air. You've got until I'm done this cig.

Thomas says you quit on bad terms.

That's accurate.

Hannah kicks Dallan in the foot. He realizes she's been doing most of the talking.

We—Dallan starts. We're hoping to find out where it comes from. The product, or whatever.

Moreno scratches his chin. I don't know that. Nobody does.

Somebody has to, Hannah says.

He drags on his cigarette. You mean the guys at the top? I don't know them, either.

We're just hoping you can tell us something, Hannah says. Anything about how it works.

Why would I do that? I've had enough trouble with all that shit.

Thomas said they really screwed you over, Hannah says.

That's an understatement. Moreno drags on the cigarette again.

What happened? Dallan asks.

Without getting into too much detail, they wanted me to do some shit I wasn't comfortable with—that no one should be okay with in my humble-ass opinion. When I told them I wouldn't, they made my life hell for a while. Until I said I wanted out. Then they let me go, but not without a warning. Moreno smiles at them wide and Dallan can see all of his front teeth, top and bottom, are too perfectly proportioned, too ominously white to be real.

Maybe this is your chance to get a little even, Dallan says.

Look, Moreno says. I don't know what you're planning, but it's a bad fucking idea. Stay away from those assholes and their business.

Just give us something, anything, and we'll leave you alone, Hannah says. Nobody has to know we talked to you. This conversation never happened. Okay?

Moreno flicks his cigarette to the ground, steps on it, and twists it out with the sole of his greasy kitchen shoe. I'll tell you this, he says, and do whatever you want with it. The guy who delivered to me, he couldn't add or subtract for shit. When he was counting out my cut, he'd always have to write the numbers out to get the math right. He'd write them down on these little scorecards from this golf course nearby. Red Pheasant Links. He would give me these little cards with my cut circled at the bottom so I could see for myself that he got it right. I swear I had dozens of them kicking around my apartment back then. I'd find them everywhere.

Alright, Hannah says. That's something? She looks at Dallan.

He shrugs. Can't say. I know the course, though.

Moreno ties his apron back around his waist. Good luck with all that, he says. It's all you're going to get from me. He fans his hands out at his waist as if to bow. Then he leaves them there by the dumpster and steps through the back kitchen door propped open by a yellow milk crate.

DEPUTY ARNASON

In the kitchen, he drapes his heavy leather jacket around a Windsor chair, collar adorned with yellowed borg lining. His wife, Joanie, is already seated at the table, back from her shift as a technician at the veterinary clinic downtown. As he takes a seat himself, she gets up, goes to the stove, and ladles out two bowls of soup for the both of them. This is their daily lunch hour routine.

In the centre of the table is a fresh focaccia from the bakery downtown and she has sliced it into inch-wide strips, perfect for dipping in the split pea soup she prepared late last night before they both went to bed. There is a vase with fresh cut geraniums she must have picked up on her walk back from work at the small Chinese grocer on the corner of Gervais Street.

She places a bowl of soup at both of their place settings. How's the rule of law today?

Same old. Car chases. Shootouts, he says. He jokes with her, but the young man from earlier that day has been weighing on his mind—that, and his conversation with Durham. His best efforts to put his head down and forget about both of them have been in vain. What about the cats and dogs?

This fourteen-year-old Beagle wouldn't stop shaking while the sedative went in. I got dog shit on my slip-ons and had to borrow Kim's backups.

He brings a spoonful to his mouth and blows the liquid cool then slurps it noisily.

He and Joanie met ten years ago. She was studying to be a veterinary technician at the community college in the next city over. He was a labourer in the oil refineries outside of Perron and worked on the routine cleaning and maintenance crews that took over during scheduled shutdowns, alternating from plant to empty plant to scrub all the floors and walls and machinery. During these periods while the regular plant workers were laid off, the town's pulse quickened and the bars were often full by the early afternoon. Some establishments even altered their opening hours to capitalize on the influx of thirsty customers looking for a distraction while the plants were closed.

He was at a local bar with the rest of his crew after the final day of a two-week job, fourteen straight twelve-hour days without a weekend, and she was at the bar studying from a textbook with a mug of beer. She caught his eye as he sat at the table ignoring his coworkers, the small sips she took between flipping pages, her occasional reach for the wooden bowl of complimentary beer nuts put out by the bartender.

He offered to buy round after round for his friends, just so he could stand beside her at the bar and place his order, hoping she might turn to him and say hello or even ask him a question. He did this five or six times without so much as a glance from her until he finally ran out of money. By this point, he'd had enough drinks to have the courage to approach her. Chatting up strangers was not something he did often—and especially not one that he found to be so beautiful and magnetic.

Instead of ordering more beer when he got to the bar, he turned to her and asked, What are you reading?

Without looking up, she replied, I'm studying.

What are you studying? His tongue lapped clumsily against the backs of his teeth as he tried to talk straight.

Proper procedure for the kitten birthing process.

So you're having kittens? he said. Congratulations.

This made her snort. I'm studying to be a vet tech.

I love animals. I always had dogs growing up. I had this one dog, a Rottweiler-golden retriever mix, and she was just the best. My dad didn't believe in vets, though. Thought it was a waste of money.

He sounds like he shouldn't have had pets.

When she got sick, he made me put her down myself with the captive bolt stunner we used on the cattle.

That's horrible, she said.

Maybe it was, he said. I think about it sometimes.

At least you had pets, she said. I wasn't allowed. My mom was allergic to just about everything with fur or feathers. It's kind of funny I'm doing what I'm doing, but I guess I always loved them—animals, I mean.

Not your parents? he said.

Jury's still out on them.

They went on that way, going back and forth and learning little things about each other, the bartender letting Arnason run up a tab in good faith on account of his being there so often. He was a loyal, honest patron with a dependable thirst. It was her final year of school and she already had work lined up for after graduation at the clinic where she'd done her job placement the summer before. He told her about how he had to climb into the huge empty tanks at the refineries with a helmet and a headlamp, an oxygen mask and a small beeper attached to his waist to detect the stinkdamp gas that would kill him in seconds if he breathed it in. He talked about all the little tricks he used to scrub at the grit and grime that had accumulated on the metal walls until they shined like new again.

When the bar closed down, they went back to her apartment and drank more beer and listened to her record collection, Ray Charles and Carly Simon and Bob Seger. He didn't know much about music, told her he never found the time to listen, but he enjoyed what she played on her record player with the built-in stereo amplifier.

A song he did know finally came on, one that used to play on the radio on days when he and his father did the farmwork and the weather was clear enough to bring electronics outside, and Arnason jumped to his feet and grabbed the floor lamp in the corner of the room, took off the shade, and began to sing along, using the bright tungsten bulb as a microphone. He stepped and shimmied around the room singing the words to her and he still remembers how she smiled at him from down on the carpet by the stereo, the yellow light outlining some of her sharp features and casting others in dark shadow. He leaned hard into the final chorus, nearly screaming the words, but tripped over the corner of the coffee table, landing face first on the bright orange bulb, snuffing out the light and filling his face and lips and the inside of his mouth with tiny shards of thin white glass.

They spent the rest of the night with a pair of tweezers, picking bits of the bulb out from the skin of his face and the gums around his bloody smile. They were married six months after that.

†

At the lunch table, Joanie asks him, Want to play a round?

Always, he says, and pulls the leather backgammon case from the shelf hidden below the tabletop. He clicks open each brass buckle and unfolds the board to the side of the geraniums. The table is small, built for two, and they can both comfortably reach their chits and dice while they go on spooning their soup. They get to work setting the black and beige pieces in their proper starting positions.

He dips a piece of bread in the green of his bowl and goes to take a bite, but when he does he thinks about the kid at the station and the story he told and he can hardly get the food down. If it comes out that this kid has a different account from the one that went down on the final police report, people will come with questions of their own. And if that happens, if things go downhill in a flash? Durham made it clear it's Arnason's ass that's on the line.

When he looks up from his lunch he sees his wife is watching him. He tries to divert his gaze back to the backgammon board and dumps his dice from their small felt-lined leather cup, but he can still feel her eyes on him. He finally looks up at her. Can I help you with something?

I was going to ask you the same thing.

I don't need anything.

I didn't say you did.

He grumbles and tries to deflect her attention back to the meal. Soup's good, he says. Can really taste that ham hock.

Is there something on your mind? his wife says.

No, Arnason says. No, just work stuff.

What stuff?

You heard about that kid, the one who overdosed at the rodeo grounds?

This woman and the cashier were whispering about it when I picked up the flowers, she says.

This weekend is always such a shit show. Every single year, goddamn.

What's Bob doing to tighten things up this time around?

Not a damn thing, he says. He's probably made it worse.

How's that?

Arnason takes a breath. He needs to calm down. I'm just talking out my ass.

It's good to talk, she says. Especially doing what you do. You need to talk.

You're right, he says. It's good. You're good.

Are you going to see your mother later today?

I'll see her for her dessert, maybe coffee.

How's she doing? Settling in any better?

For what we're paying, she should feel like the Queen of fucking England.

I know it's a lot. But what can we do? She's only got a few years left.

Don't talk like that, he says. He stares into his soup.

I don't know what else you want me to say about it. It's the truth, hon, and in her state, with all the spills she took in her own place at the end there, how confused she gets, we need to get her the best care we can afford. She deserves to be comfortable.

I know that.

It's a good situation for her. She deserves it. We owe it to her.

I'm not sure we can go on paying for it if she doesn't kick it in the next twelve months.

We'll find the money. We'll cut back.

I'm trying to scrape some stuff together, he says. Some extra work on the side.

What kind of work?

Grunt stuff. Martens told me I could help him with his tree removal this summer, but I don't want that peanut for a boss. I don't know. I'll figure something out.

Joanie reaches across the table, over the backgammon board and past the vase of flowers and the bread, and she rests her hand on his. It is smaller and smoother than his and he feels the coolness of her taut fingers temper his own, thick and red and full of blood.

DALLAN DERMOTT

Hannah is seated across from him at Burger Boss. She picks at fries in a wax paper bag and dips them in a pool of ketchup on a sandwich wrapper. It is a scene he could not have predicted, not even earlier that morning as he made his way to the police station where he would ultimately fail to right the wrong he had committed last night. And she watched him do it, kill a person she cared about so much, and yet they are together in this fast food joint on the northern fringe of the place they call home, starting off towards some ill-formed and elusive idea of justice or redemption. That takes trust and he's grateful he might be gaining it from her, little by little.

He's finished his food and sucks at the dregs of his Coke hidden amongst the crushed ice in the bottom of his cup. What are we going to do when we get to the course? he asks.

We're just going to take a look around, see what we can find. She talks through a mouthful of french fries and ketchup, visibly more comfortable around him since he first showed up at her door.

What if we actually do see someone? Or you know, find something?

She sips her drink and swallows it down. Haven't thought that far ahead yet.

Maybe we should take a second now to think it through? Make a plan.

Come on, she says. Let's go.

Before he can agree or disagree, she's up and heading for the door. Dallan takes both of their plastic trays and dumps the empty wrappers and food refuse into the receptacle on their way out.

†

They drive along the storefronts in the long parking lot of the commercial block until they reach the north exit. Hannah signals right to go to the intersection that will take them out onto the highway, but there is something Dallan knows he needs to do. If not now, in the surreal wake still churning around this newly altered life, then he might never have the courage.

Wait, he says to her. Can you make a left really quick?

Golf course is that way? she says. She gestures down the highway where there are only level fields and rural acreage homes and, further on, the worst golf course in the entire area, Red Pheasant Links.

I want to make a quick stop.

Where?

Brooks's place. He lives around the corner there. His parents do.

You sure? she asks.

Just a quick stop, he says. I promise.

Hannah flicks her signal up and then makes a left turn into another subdivision. A few houses down, she makes a right into a small cul-de-sac called Bellerose of only a dozen or so homes.

It's that one, Dallan says. The burgundy house with the black trim.

In the driveway is Brooks's parents' like-new SUV and the older, rustier Ford Ranger single cab that Brooks used to drive, first to school and more recently to his job selling suits and ties and dress shirts at a chain menswear store downtown. Dallan wanted Brooks to come with him to college—he had the grades and could take out a student loan—but Brooks said he didn't feel like he belonged, that he'd be like a sci-fi character dropped into the middle of a rich white teen drama.

Hannah pulls in behind the Ranger and Dallan opens his door. With one foot out, he asks, You coming?

Should I?

Not if you don't want to, he says.

She takes a deep breath and then steps out of the sedan.

The air is hot and dry. Dallan can remember only rain, sheets and sheets of it, in all his years of attending the Sunsetter. He remembers black mud, sometimes up to his ankles in the paths through the field around the grandstand and corral, mucking up his boots on the way to get a better look at the bareback broncs and bucking bulls with the terrified looks in their eyes. He remembers the time Brooks's runner got caught in the soupy mess behind the bleachers. He had a habit of never tying his shoes and it slipped clean off as he walked. He didn't have time to react as he took his next step and planted his socked foot down into the cold mud and rainwater.

Hannah and Dallan climb the porch to the front door in lockstep and he reaches for the bell. He hesitates ever so slightly, wonders if Hannah has noticed, and then pushes it. At first, he hears nothing from inside the house. Then the familiar pattering of Brooks's yellow lab builds from down the hall to right behind the closed door. She stops there and begins to bark.

The front door always sticks a little, the wood swelled since it was installed by Brooks's father some five years before, and the person on the other side has to heave on it once or twice before it finally opens up.

Brooks's mother looks exhausted, sallow. Her eyes are swollen and red. She hardly seems to register the two of them on her doorstep. The dog forces her head from back between her legs and snorts and pants. After a too-long, uncomfortable silence, Brooks's mother speaks. Dallan, she says.

Hi, Bridge, he says. He's always called her Bridge, short for Bridget.

Would you like to come in?

No, he says. No, I don't think I can. He can't imagine now entering the house he spent so many years visiting.

She nods and pushes her lips into an unconvincing smile.

Dallan avoids her eyes. I'm sorry, he says. He feels the heat of tears building behind his eyes.

Sorry for what? she asks.

Brooks, I guess. For what happened to him.

Some part of everything that has transpired, if not all of it, somehow feels like his fault. He imagines himself walking into the road and lying down over the dotted yellow line until a car or a truck comes along to take his guilt away for good.

Dallan, she says. Why don't you come in for a minute? I'll get you and your friend something cold to drink.

Dallan turns to Hannah. Her face doesn't change, neither agreeing nor declining, and so he accepts Bridget's invitation out of respect. They follow her down the hallway to the kitchen. The dog pokes at the backs of their legs with the point of her snout. There is a photograph of Bridge and David, from before they had their sons, standing in front of a townhome in the Little Jamaica neighbourhood, in the city where they met. Dallan has heard the story a dozen times or more, of how they left their friends and family behind so David could take a job during the oil boom, so they could try for a better life for their infant sons, half a country away from everyone and everything they knew or loved.

As they come into the kitchen, Bridget speaks again, slowly at first. David is in our bedroom upstairs getting some rest. We were at the hospital all night. They sent us home to sleep early this morning. I don't know why we stayed. It's not like they gave him a room. Bridget is sort of rambling, speaking her words into the air, not at anyone in particular. Of course, she says, They told us there was nothing we could do. We knew that. Of course we did. But we wanted to stay close to him as long as we could, even if that meant being there outside that awful place they kept him in, down in the basement.

Bridget opens the fridge and removes the same glass pitcher of deep red sorrel tea that is always waiting for guests inside. She pours two cups, hands them to Dallan and Hannah. No ice, no fresh citrus split over the rim as Dallan has come to expect from Bridge.

In the living room, they sit on the tufted leather loveseat opposite the fireplace. On the mantle are photos of the entire family, on vacation or in the department store studio for professional portraits, a family that counted four up until only hours ago. There are photos of Brooks and his younger brother, Aaron, arms draped weakly around each other's shoulders, trophies for the team sports the boys took part in over the years and a plaque for academic achievement that Brooks was awarded in the first year of high school, before he stopped caring about the things he began to think were trivial and of little consequence. He only kept up with basketball because, as a Black kid in a mostly white town, he never really felt the choice was his. He told Dallan he always felt he couldn't miss a party in his sophomore year because everyone expected him to be there. Dallan never judged this, never felt the need to. Right up until Brooks drew his last breath, he enjoyed those things fully—the beers, the girl in the woods with her hand on the buckle of his belt, the little round white pills he insisted he pay for.

He and Hannah are careful and still with the tea cupped in their laps. Bridget sits on the end of a chair in the corner of the room, leaning forward, her arms stiff and awkward, her back curved upward. There is no sign of Aaron anywhere in the house. Dallan wonders if he received the news last night, if he decided not to come home at all when he did.

The room is tense. Its wood panel walls do not exude the same warmth they had for Dallan the countless times he visited before. The green shag carpet itches his feet through his socks.

Finally he asks Bridget, Do you want to know what happened?

She does not answer. She tries to hold back her sobs at first, blowing them out in small bursts like an uncontainable force trying to escape her from the inside, and then she surrenders. Tears streak her face and her chest heaves with each bawl as she holds her eyes on the mantle, the only part of her that keeps still as her body convulses.

Hannah goes down the hallway, returns with a wad of toilet paper and offers it to Bridget. She accepts it without a word, dabs her eyes and cheeks and then blows her nose.

With her eyes still locked on the mantle she says, I think it's best I join David and get some rest.

Of course. I'll come back around. Tomorrow?

Maybe Monday, love.

Bridget walks them back to the door. In the entranceway, she extends a hand to Dallan and wraps her small fingers around his. With her thumb, she rubs the spot on his wrist where one might normally check for a pulse. He and Hannah walk out in silence and she closes the door delicately behind them.

Dallan stands still and stares out into Bellerose cul-de-sac, not registering any details, any single car or colour or tree, but rather all of it at once, like the smears on a painter's palette at the final completion of a new work. Seeing Bridge has only made Brooks's death feel more dreamlike and, at the same time, more painful.

We should get going, Hannah says.

He breathes out, whistling a single note, low and wavering through his lips, and then follows her back to the car. He pauses before he bends down through the passenger door. He cranes his head over the top of the car to look at Hannah, maybe to thank her, but she has already taken up her place in the driver's seat.

HANNAH FIELDS

S he waits in the intersection for the light to change to yellow, for her turn to make a left onto the highway heading north. It has always startled her how abruptly their town gives way to fields of wheat and corn, to pastures and to small, isolated convenience stores advertising game jerky and bottle rockets, the occasional home framed by stark conifers standing precariously against the open sky. The golf course is only about a ten-minute drive, but even that short expanse is refreshing compared to the rows of houses, the downtown condos, and the strip malls, each with their own offerings of liquor, gas, and groceries.

Dallan hasn't said a word since they left Brooks's porch and she can't blame him. She imagines she would feel the same, standing there in such a familiar place, now with its most significant point of association erased from the world. How Brooks's mother stared and muttered reminded her of her own mother in a small way. Only that, if she had died like Brooks had, her mother would probably be walking the aisles of the grocery store cornering people for meandering conversation, begging them to share in her grief. Hannah is different from her mother in this way. She keeps quiet, holds her emotions in. She knows there must be a limit to how much she can retain behind her stony facade before it all forces its way through the cracks or spills over the lip. That point, she has never reached.

She fiddles with the knob on the stereo until she's found a volume that matches the whir of the wind rushing around them and the groan of the engine beneath the hood. All of it becomes one wall of sound, one undivided song.

The sun is still out, eyeing up the sky's edge, and the turnoff sign for Red Pheasant Links is backlit by its orange glow. She turns off the highway and into the parking lot. It is mostly empty, save for a few trucks and cars parked right in front of the clubhouse. In all her years driving up and down that road on her way to her grandparents' farm, or else on hunting or fishing trips with her father, she has never seen more than one or two golf carts out on the links. Even now, in the parking lot, all but one cart space is occupied by rain-battered beige vehicles.

She parks at the far end of the gravel lot, closest to the highway, under the shade of a stand of pines. They exit the vehicle and walk across to the clubhouse, a rectangle building with immaculate off-white siding, probably the only upgrade the entire place has seen in years.

They approach the front desk, but there is no one behind it. On the walls are yellowing posters of former pros and below them dusty rental clubs lean against each other in scuffed golf bags. There is a bell on the counter and she rings it once. Its sound is harsh in the relative quiet of the empty office, though just down the hall of the clubhouse she can hear a few patrons in the bar, the occasional clink of two glasses, the swelling voices of old men now and again telling their friends an anecdote or a prefab joke.

A woman comes from the back room. Her hair is dyed an unnatural shade of bright red with blond highlights down the front bangs. What're you doing here? she says to them, her voice scratchy and low.

We'd like to play nine holes, she says. With rentals.

And a cart, Dallan says.

Can't. We're closing early today. Fifteen minutes from now.

But it's beautiful out, Hannah says. It won't be dark for another three hours at least.

Maintenance, says the woman. We always plan maintenance during Sunsetter. Most of our regulars are off at the grounds. She brings her hand to her mouth as if holding an invisible bottle, tilts her head back in a mock chug. You know, she says.

Seriously?

Did I stutter, hon?

Hannah scrunches her face in frustration, nods sarcastically to the woman, and begins to walk away. Dallan follows her and they exit the clubhouse. She leads them around the corner to where the carts are parked in an awkward row, some straight and neat along the curb, others backed in on angles lacking any and all sense or harmony.

Well shit, Dallan says. What do you think we should do?

I mean, she says. Then she stops to think. We could just walk out there. Who would know? She's probably the only one working.

He looks around. There are empty metal drums rusting in one corner of the parking lot, an old dilapidated mower near-buried in the tall grass that has been allowed to grow around it and beneath it, unchecked, since the snow thawed several months back.

This place is a real shithole, he says. Maintenance, my ass.

Hannah can tell Dallan is emerging, however slowly, from the cold shock of their visit to Brooks's. She remembers little of him from school, though one characteristic that does stand out in her memory is his awkward nature. After seeing what he saw last night, after doing what he did, she can hardly believe he is out in the world at all right now. She is glad she can be a point of human connection for him, and maybe in time he can be that for her. She's been alone for so long in the world. In truth, it's always been a caustic place without the company of others, even if she tells herself she prefers it that way.

They dip down the path through the line of trees beyond the parking lot, careful to look back and check the window on the side of the building in case the woman with the wild hair is peeking out. They tiptoe out onto the empty green of the eighteenth and final hole, lumpy with patches of dead brown grass, and cut across to the lopsided fairway that rolls unevenly with old growth roots and other impurities beneath what should be a manicured surface.

What are we looking for, you think? Dallan says.

Anything out of the ordinary, I guess.

This entire place is out of the ordinary. It's giving me the fucking creeps.

They walk at a slow pace. The course is quiet, save for the occasional click of a bug in the tall grass of the ditch or a lone car passing on the highway over to their left. They come to a water trap that feeds off draining stormwater on rainy days, the final obstacle of the hole. At its bottom are rocks covered in a green slime. Now there are only trace amounts of runoff collected between a few lost balls and unkempt weeds and they cross over on a bridge of cinder blocks and weathered two-by-fours to the other side.

She wants to coax Dallan further out of his shell, so she asks the first question that comes to mind. What have you been doing since high school? She's immediately embarrassed by her own dull predictability.

He pauses, bashful, before he answers. Nothing I'd say that's worth talking about. More school.

What are you studying?

General stuff right now. I don't know what I want to do, but my dad forced me to apply, and when I got in, he told me he'd kick me out if I didn't take classes. He didn't care which ones, just that I was enrolled.

Your dad's a hard ass?

I wouldn't say that. He was never rough or anything. He always told me he values an education or whatever. It's like he feels less guilty as a parent knowing I'm doing what I'm supposed to be. But what about you? Where've you been since grad?

I've been working—at the massage therapy clinic downtown. Living at home and saving. We were going to try and get a place next month.

You and who?

She looks at him. Nick, she says.

Right, Dallan says.

He keeps his eyes to the ground. She watches him watch his own shadow passing over the grass. It's clear that nobody has ever taught him how to console a person, how to come to their aid in any situation beyond a minor physical injury. It's something she thinks must be true for all young men. All the ones she's met, anyway.

Dallan keeps on as if everything is fine. Did he live around here?

He didn't really live anywhere. He's been with Carlsbad for the past two years now. You know, the production company that does the Sunsetter midway.

And they go from place to place all year long?

Exactly. Northern fairs are in the spring and summer, and then they go south when it gets too cold. He was going to stay this time, though. Stay in Perron, I mean.

Dallan puts his hand on her shoulder, but pulls it away almost as quickly as she's able to notice it there at all.

They make it to the tee for the eighteenth hole, a raised mound of grass with a patch of badly beaten turf and white two-by-fours rising crookedly up a foot from the dirt on either side. They follow the gravel path, walk between the hard ruts carved out by the wheels of the carts. They wind past a garbage bin overflowing with aluminum cans and brown glass bottles. Through a break in the trees, Hannah can see a red flag emblazoned with a white number seventeen.

The green is closed in by tall pines on three sides, but opens up to the fairway, which bends around another stand of trees obscuring the tee-off point. At the back of the green is a small sand trap, still neatly groomed after a full Saturday of supposed golfing, and they walk around it to the green.

Dallan bends down and unties his shoes. He steps on each heel with the opposite toe and pries them off his feet, does the same with his socks. Ever done this? he says.

Taken my shoes off?

No, he laughs. Walked barefoot on the green. Brooks and I used to do this every time we went golfing with our dads. We even snuck out of my place one night and rode our bikes out to the course on the east side. They'd just watered the greens and we drank beers and walked in circles for an hour. There's something about it, especially when it's a little damp. It's the best grass you'll ever walk on.

She crouches to unbuckle her sandals, lifts her heels, and points her toes. They slip from her feet. She walks out onto the short green grass and it feels as though she is walking in a shallow puddle of water, all of the dense sprouts coming together to form something close to a liquid substance. Her whole body feels lighter. The hairs stand up, shudder on her arms and the back of her neck. Then a noise catches her attention—the rumble of a gas motor off in the distance, down the seventeenth fairway and around the trees.

You hear that?

I hear it, Dallan says.

I didn't see any balls out there. Did you?

It's getting louder. Heading this direction.

Both of them scramble to put their shoes back on. Dallan shoves his socks into the pocket of his jeans. Come on, he says. He leads her into the woods that surround the green and they both crouch low behind a juniper bush.

Her pulse has jumped. Her nose stings with the smell of the leaves and the fresh spring buds in the scrub. Let's just go. We can walk back along the highway to the car.

We're good here, he says. They won't see us.

Come on, Dallan, she pleads. Let's go.

His eyes remain focussed on the approaching golf cart. Let's wait them out and then we'll leave.

DALLAN DERMOTT

He is crouched down, his tall frame folded in. He can feel the
dampness in the air collected in the shade beneath the pine
boughs. His breathing is shallow, quick. Hannah kneels down
beside him and he tries to peer through the gaps in the foliage to
get a better view of the approaching golf cart.

It peels around the bend in the fairway past the distant stand
of trees, before slowing down and putting along towards the
seventeenth green. The two golfers do not stop to play. Instead,
they head straight for the green where he and Hannah have just
been stepping around in their bare feet. On the highway behind
them, only ten or so feet, a long-haul engine roars past and makes
Dallan's breath jump and catch in the back of his throat. As the
cart approaches, the two men come into focus.

Think they're employees? Hannah asks.

They don't look like they work here.

They don't look like they're golfing, either. It's supposed to be
closed right now anyway.

Both the men in the golf cart are in blue jeans. One of them wears a starchy black windbreaker and the other, a borg-lined leather jacket much too heavy for the heat, not the preppy shorts and collared shirts normally indicative of someone playing a round or working at the course. They pull around the green and park along the treeline beside the sand trap.

Dallan tenses. He recognizes one of the men. It's the officer from the station, the one who questioned him earlier that morning, who warned him to keep quiet about what had really happened with Nick at the Sunsetter. He can feel his arms tremble and quake as they struggle to hold his body weight up. He wants to run.

What? Hannah whispers.

Him, he says, gestures at the one in the leather jacket. I know him.

Hannah squints harder, repositions her head to get a better view of the two men. Who is he?

They are close now, within earshot. Dallan does not answer. It isn't golf bags they have on the back of their cart but a single spade shovel. The other man takes it up and steps down into the pit of sand while the officer watches from the edge.

Neither Dallan nor Hannah speak as they watch the man in the pit stab his spade into the sand in various places, testing the firmness of the ground. He stops, his shovel half-buried, and shimmies it around, twisting metal in the sand. He starts to dig.

The officer looks around the green for any signs of activity. He seems alert, maybe even a little paranoid, his head on a swivel. Still, he has an official, serious air. He is tight-lipped and expressionless.

After a few shovelfuls, the man in the sand trap bends down and pulls up what appears to be a black bag. It looks like the one Dallan brings camping to keep his clothing and supplies dry. He dusts the sand off its smooth surface and hands it up to the officer. The man takes the rake from the rough grass at the edge of the trees and levels the surface of the sand until it's impeccable again.

They both get back into the golf cart. The engine turns over and they back out, tires spinning out on the turf. They take off down the path in the direction of the clubhouse.

HANNAH FIELDS

In the empty parking lot at Red Pheasant Links, the interior of her mother's car has warmed and the smell of the dusty upholstery is heavy. She sits in the driver's seat and Dallan slumps beside her. She is clenched all over, overwhelmed by the feeling that what they saw was not meant to be seen. If they had been found there spying from the brush, she's sure that whatever might have happened would've been bad for them. She turns the key in the ignition part way so she can roll down the windows and allow the fresh air to waft inside.

Dallan leans forward in his bucket seat. He rolls his fingers on the glove box, making a small and hollow tapping noise with each tip. He does this over and over again and each time it seems to grow louder in Hannah's head. She glares at his nervous hands as they fumble around in front of him.

Would you quit that? she says.

He pulls his hands in close to his body and folds them on his lap. He leans back in his seat. Sorry, he says.

That could have been so, so bad back there, she says. It was too close.

There's no way they would have seen us.

She blows a sarcastic puff of air. You had to take your shoes off for your stupid ritual.

What are you talking about? You did it, too. I was just trying to lighten up the mood a bit. I thought we were having fun.

You think this is fun? There's nothing fun about any of this.

Look, he says. I'm sorry about the shoe thing. It was stupid.

It's like, what the fuck are we even doing? I don't even know you. Why are we doing this?

Hold up. It was your idea to talk to your brother and his sketchy friend. Isn't that the reason we came out here?

I don't want to do this.

Then why are you here?

Do you know why we're out here? The actual reason why we're out here? Hannah hits the steering wheel with the palms of her hands. Because you killed my fucking boyfriend.

Your boyfriend? Was he even your boyfriend? My best friend got killed by your so-called boyfriend—and you hardly even fucking knew the guy. He was gone all year with a goddamn carnival.

Dallan's voice is raised to a level she hadn't imagined him capable of. She rises to meet him.

I knew him better than anyone. I fucking *loved* him.

You met him one time, Dallan says. I knew Brooks my entire life. He was family to me. He was all I had and your loser boyfriend killed him with his fucking pills.

Are you serious? Both of you went to him to buy your shit and you took it willingly. Don't pretend to me right now that you didn't know what could happen. Don't play dumb. It's in the news every goddamn day.

Dallan throws his hands in the air. I can't believe we're even having this conversation. Nick was just some guy you fucked once. An entire year ago. And then he strung you along. What did you do, text each other every day? That's not a relationship. You talk about all these plans you had? I bet he would've been gone with the rest of them on Monday.

Yeah? she says. Her eyebrows raise and she breaks. Thanks to you I'll never know. She begins to cry. She allows herself to heave and rock as the sobs take hold of her entire body.

Dallan's face is in his hands. He is shaking his head. Hannah, he says. Look, Hannah, I'm sorry. I didn't mean it.

She sits up straight to catch her breath. Then what did you mean?

I don't know. I was angry. I don't get angry. I didn't know what I was saying. I was just saying whatever came into my head.

Well, I was serious. Her sobbing has subdued. She pats her cheeks and eyes dry with the sleeve of her shirt. From the centre console, she removes a package of tissues and blows her nose. We'll never know if he was going to stay or what that could have been like. I'll never get to know.

Dallan unbuckles his seatbelt and leans across the centre console. He wraps his arms around her and he holds her and she presses her face into the shoulder of his shirt. Her breath collects there, warm and moist, and for a moment she draws in the air of her own exhalations. A calm begins to come over her.

I'm sorry, he says to her. He repeats himself over and over. His voice is low and even. I am. For you—he would have stayed.

She hears him. She chooses to believe him, this person, closer to her now than most have ever come. She heaves, once, twice, and then sniffles her nose clear. She wipes it on his shirt and looks him in the eyes. I got snot on your shirt, she says.

It's seen worse.

She does her best to wipe Dallan's shoulder clean. She takes a deep breath and flutters her eyelashes to dry them, runs the side of her finger underneath. Then she looks through the windshield at the clubhouse. The woman from behind the counter stands on the front deck with her back to them, locking the door. When she turns, she stops and stares their car down. She holds her gaze and does not move for some time.

Both Hannah and Dallan watch her, motionless.

We should go, Hannah says. She rubs her eyes once more and clears her throat.

She starts the car and then pulls out of the parking lot. In the rearview mirror, Hannah can see the woman watch them disapprovingly until they turn onto the highway and leave her behind.

DEPUTY ARNASON

He rides shotgun on the way back into town from Red Pheasant Links. They drive in a civilian car, Martens's decade-old brown sedan. He locked the package in the trunk before they left the parking lot, but it still feels like it's in the cab with him, heavy in his lap. He sometimes feels this way, that his side job manifests itself like phantom weight or pain, regardless of whether he's currently in the act of it or not. He buries the thought like a dead pet.

They turn off the highway into downtown. You want me to drop you at your mother's? Martens asks.

Sure. Do that.

How's she doing?

She's okay. It's alright in there. They've got communal areas with big screen TVs and shuffleboard and all that bullshit.

You eaten the food there?

I've joined her for a few meals.

Isn't it all goop and crap? Porridge and jello and mashed whatever?

Most of them have dentures, Martens. They can still eat whatever they want.

So what did you try off the menu?

Last time it was pot roast. Mashed potatoes. Peas and carrots. A little gravy and some fresh rolls. You know, regular homey stuff. It tastes alright. It's the smell I can't get past.

What's it smell like?

You know that dog food factory that used to be south of here?

How could I forget? Martens makes a face like he's just breathed it in again, the smell of the slurry of butcher throwaways being processed into kibble. I know what you're dealing with, though. Places like that, those long-term care facilities, they cost a fortune. I know it firsthand.

Arnason nods, his eyes on the highway ahead.

When Andrea's father was dealing with the Alzheimer's, we put him in the same home our mom's in. We damn-near had to take out a second mortgage to keep him alive.

You're telling me.

And for what? The old man didn't even recognize me, never mind his own daughter near the end of it.

It's the right thing to do, Arnason says. The humane thing.

It's goddamn criminal how much it costs doing the right thing sometimes. You think for all we do for our country, tax-paying members of this society like we are, they'd foot the bill to keep us comfortable and alive when we can't work no more. Is that too much to ask?

Why do you think we both agreed to all this shit? Arnason gestures a thumbs-up towards the back of the car.

You need the money. I need the money. We all need the fucking money.

But a sheriff, though, Arnason says.

Apparently that's an entirely different circumstance, Martens says. He takes the exit off the highway, towards downtown. Has Durham ever taken you out to his place on Skeleton Lake?

He has.

And the boat he's got out there? All those fucking five-point bucks and bear skins and shit. I'll never have anything like that in my entire life. No chance in hell.

I don't know a thing about boats.

His is probably about a twenty-eight-footer. Two outboard motors, all brand new. That thing probably costs more than my house. The stereo system he's got on there is better than the one in the theatre downtown.

Arnason scoffs. Makes me think he's getting a significantly better cut than we are in all this.

I'm still going to be paying for it in therapy after I retire. This shit, it keeps me up at night. I just roll from my belly to my back with my eyes closed thinking about little white tablets. Eyes open—little white tablets. Eyes closed—little white tablets.

Arnason nods along. Sometimes even Martens can make a little sense. As they approach the next intersection, the long white arms of the railway crossing begin to flash red and descend, barring the road.

You know what's good money? Martens says. Waste removal. People pay a ton to get rid of their garbage.

I don't want to be a garbageman.

I knew this guy, Bernie Arnaud. He had this ugly fucking couch, had it in his garage because he couldn't stand to keep it in the house anymore. It was this greenish-brown colour, like baby shit. The same colour as your wife's eyes, Arnason.

What the fuck are you saying?

Good colour on a woman's whites, don't get me wrong, but an ugly fucking colour for a couch.

Arnason shakes his head. They've worked together for half a decade and he's become acutely attuned to when his partner is about to go on a tangent. His stories, long and meandering and often pointless, have echoed in his ears during so many night shifts and dull patrols. The brand of banality that Martens embodies is one of a handful of things that can truly infuriate Arnason.

Martens goes on. Bernie wants to get rid of this couch, wash his hands of the thing, but he doesn't want to pay the fee to throw it away properly. Bernie's old fashioned, you know? When a guy's got something he doesn't have use for anymore, he should be able to dispose of it, no questions asked. This is Bernie's thinking anyways.

Arnason can do nothing but listen, his eyes glossed over, fixed on the road. The trains at this particular crossing can be dozens or even hundreds of cars long and they go real slow as they move through the city. He thinks about getting out of the car and walking to the care home on the shoulder of the road.

There's another part to Bernie Arnaud being old fashioned, Martens says. He wants to get rid of this couch, but he can't give it away because of the colour of the thing. He can't just leave it on the curb if nobody wants it. He'd have to see it every time he left his house, and plus, there are steep fines for dumping. Waste companies won't take it, not without a hefty fee—and Bernie won't pay it. But he devises a way to get it to them anyway.

Bernie goes out into his garage and finds his hacksaw. He's old fashioned, you see, so there wasn't going to be any power tools involved. Only Bernie, his hacksaw, and that ugly fucking couch. He gets to cutting it up, first in bigger pieces, halves and the halves of those halves. He cuts it into quarters and eighths. The pieces keep getting smaller, and he starts loading the stuffing and springs into green garbage bags. He loads the pieces up, too, once they're about the sizes of apples and oranges. Bernie cuts that green bastard into as many pieces as he can and throws *them* out onto the curb instead. Next day the waste company picks them up like anything else.

So what are you saying?

Shit, he says. I had a point I was going to make. I just lost my train of thought.

Is that a pun?

I wasn't trying to be funny. It just comes to me naturally, I guess.

If the Bernies of the world are out there refusing to pay, Arnason says, then why the fuck would I want to be a garbageman?

The end of the train cars passes and the barrier lifts to let them through. They bounce over the lip onto the bridge, the sound of road beneath the tires jumping a register from the asphalt to the concrete. It is a hazy, brown river that separates the middle of Perron, wide and shallow from decades of gnawing at its own banks, the soil made loose by years of deforestation to make room for farms that were themselves eventually graded and paved, replaced by the budding condos and commercial real estate. The river has made a deep and gradual valley in the otherwise flat earth and the heart of downtown runs parallel to the slow-moving water.

Martens pulls up three blocks from the station in front of the nursing home. Arnason gets out. He tips his hat to his partner, glad to be rid of him for even a little while, and lets him know he'll be back at the station in a half-hour—an hour at most—to do their usual deliveries.

It's convenient that his mother's facility is only three blocks from work—but that is about the only thing he can think of as a positive in the situation. She is dying of simple, unavoidable age, the failing of the oldest cells in her body, and that gradual descent has her confused in both the deepest and most commonplace corners of her mind. In January, she woke in the night and went to boil water for a pot of tea. In the process, she knocked the pot off and scalded her thighs, shins, and feet. The accident put her in the hospital for the month that followed and when she was deemed healthy enough to leave it was the care home that she went to next.

Arnason tries the front door of the facility and forgets it's locked. The door stays barred so patrons don't wander out into the street. If they want to leave the building, they need a nurse for supervision. It makes him feel low, things coming full circle like that, a person born helplessly into the world and then helplessly waiting until they are permitted by modern medicine to leave it.

He presses the buzzer for the front desk and announces himself as Mr. Arnason, Marge's son. He gets an affirmative from the receptionist and the door buzzes, unlocks itself.

Inside, he wipes his boots on the rug in the foyer. The cafeteria is straight down the main hall and the entire building smells like the steam of their most recent collective meal, the dark brown mush of it. He's come to associate this smell with his mother's decline.

There are still a number of folks at their tables, finishing the last of their meals or else hunched over a bowl of custard and a cup of something hot. He scans the room for his mother but has a hard time making out one shock of white hair for another. He walks between the tables until he's sure he's had a good look at everyone, convinced his mother is not among them.

Back down the main hallway in the foyer and reception area, there is an old man on a bench by the front door. He waves Arnason down before he can make a right to his mother's room. The man is sunken and liver-spotted and beckons Arnason closer.

Are you here to take me for my cigarette?

His voice is crushed rock. Arnason waves his hand at him. No, sorry. I don't work here.

The man frowns at him. I'd like to go for my cigarette now.

I'm sure someone will be by soon. Arnason looks around for a nurse, gives the man a shrug.

Down the hall, there are doors on both sides and some of them are open, patrons inside being tended to by staff or else sitting in armchairs by windows or alone at the foot of their single beds. Others are closed and when he arrives at his mother's room he sees that hers is as well. He knocks.

Mom? He says her name into the hard surface of the door.

He can hear the weak sound of a voice on the other side, but he can't quite make out the words. Unlike the front entrance, the doors to the individual rooms are never locked, also a point of the safety procedure, and so he opens it and peers in. As usual, his mother is in her maroon armchair by the window that looks out onto the seating area in the yard behind the building. Outside, he can see a stream of cars and trucks going steadily by beyond the tall hedges of Canadian hemlock that close the area in. Even the traffic is worse during Sunsetter.

His mother has a book closed on her lap, one of her illustrated encyclopedias, and she smiles at him as he bends down through the door.

He sits on the edge of the bed opposite of her. He does not take his coat off. It's a strange thing he's come to understand, to see someone you know as well as your mother fade and shrink into a stranger, to look into her eyes and to feel something other than at home in them. She has become frail since her accident, too scared or ashamed of her own shortcomings to look at him. She stares at the space on the carpet just beyond the tops of her knees and chews at the insides of her cheeks—a habit she's had for as long as he can remember.

How you doing, Mom?

Oh, she says, still without eye contact. Well.

Did you get your coffee and dessert?

I didn't want supper.

You're not supposed to skip meals. You know that. They're going to bring it to you in here now. You hate that. They'll be knocking on your door any second and coming inside and disrupting your Marge-time.

Fuck 'em, she says.

She keeps on chewing at her cheeks, staring off. He feels it will be a short visit today.

Can I go get it for you?

Get what?

Your dinner, Ma.

I'm not hungry.

They're going to bring it anyway. You need to eat.

I don't care. I'm not hungry.

Fine, he says. I'm not going to force you. He reaches a hand out to her and places it lightly on her knee. I've got a feeling it might be a few days before I can make it back here to visit. Work's been busy.

She nods and chews, nods and chews.

I've just got a feeling is all.

Then she reaches her own cupped hand, streaked with the blue of her protruding veins, and places it over his forearm, rests it on the skin under the rolled sleeve of his shirt. She lifts her head and looks at him, right into his eyes, and she smiles. Sweetness, she says. Will I see you tomorrow?

I'll try, Mom, he says. But I can't say.

HANNAH FIELDS

The music in Thomas's apartment is all bass. She can feel it in her chest, beating against her ribs in metred gusts. She sits beside Dallan on the same couch where they sat earlier that day, and all around is a haze of smoke from cigarettes and joints that Thomas's friends have lit inside. She figures there are thirty people crammed into the small one-bedroom apartment, maybe even forty.

She cracks open the beer Dallan brought her from the kitchen. It's cold and crisp and, after a morning and an afternoon that has so far felt like several days, driving around town with a near-stranger, chasing something she's not sure she even wants to find, she has developed a thirst. The beer goes down smooth and quick, the small bubbles of carbonation bursting on the roof of her mouth and her tongue and throat. She wants so badly to rid her body of the fear that still grips it from the near miss at the golf course, and of the grief that has lingered all day like a phantom cord tethering her to the earth, making every movement a trial.

It's early for so much pace at a party, so much energy, but the bands at the Sunsetter beer gardens go on at seven and are wrapped by midnight. For this weekend every May, people start their drinking early. Everyone at Thomas's is trying to keep up with each other, tying one on for Saturday night, and their inhibitions are fading.

Thomas plays host, floats from circle to circle of friends laughing and yelling over the noise of the party. Even with his help today, she can hardly look at him without feeling resentment towards the mess he's made of his life, the way he revels in it. She wants more from him. It's also his absence that she's bitter towards—the support or advice he never offered, the shelter he never gave, all the things she imagines she might have experienced growing up with a different brother, maybe one more like Dallan and less like him.

She swallows the last quarter of her can. One more? she asks Dallan.

Dallan smiles weakly. He's been stiff, a bundle of nerves and clenched cartilage all day, and just when he seemed to be pulling out of it, she lashed out at him in the parking lot and made it worse. It's like he's reverted back to the morning and all the time between them has been erased. She goes back to the kitchen and returns with two more cans.

How long are we going to be here? Dallan asks.

It's six-thirty now. The first couple bands are usually pretty forgettable. I bet Thomas will lead everyone over in an hour or so? She leans forward and picks up a pack of cigarettes from the coffee table. You smoke?

Dallan shrugs. She turns the pack over and slides out a lighter and a couple king-sized cigarettes. He takes one, puts it between his lips and she holds the flame from the lighter to the tip until it cherries. She does the same and inhales deeply, fills her lungs with heat. She holds the smoke down in her chest, then exhales out her nostrils.

The familiar feeling of heaviness comes over her, a pulling that she remembers from late summer nights out on the empty high school soccer fields, camping trips spent around bonfires with friends before they graduated and went their separate ways. She and Dallan drag on the cigarettes in silence, side-by-side. Thomas walks over to them, making his rounds, and takes the pack from in front of Hannah. He pulls one out for himself, lights up. His chin bobs up and down with a magpie-like energy.

So, he says between huffs, you two still looking to roll tonight?

Is your hook-up here? Hannah asks.

Thomas gestures over to the corner where a guy is having a conversation with a girl. He looks normal enough to Hannah, his black t-shirt tucked into his jeans with a worn brown leather belt around his waist. That's him? she says. She doesn't know what she was expecting, whether she thought Thomas's dealer would have a particularly sinister look, like an Eastern European mobster from a bad action movie or a decrepit farm kid from the meth-cooking TV shows.

He's waiting for a re-up. Busy week, I guess. He told me he's meeting his supplier some place nearby real soon now. Should I put your order in?

Please do, Dallan says.

Please do, Thomas repeats. This kid is a fucking narc.

Dallan turns red in the face. He shakes his head, quick and nervous. I'm not, he says.

Thomas laughs and punches him in the shoulder.

Hannah rolls her eyes. Just let us know when we're good to go, she says. Tell us what we owe you.

Thomas nods again, his head still bobbing with pendulum consistency. He floats away into his cramped apartment.

DEPUTY ARNASON

He and Martens inch into the alleyway behind the strip mall. His window is down and he can smell the old fryer oil collected in the black vats behind the restaurants. The road is uneven with haphazardly patched potholes and he dips right like a boxer dodging a jab as the passenger side sinks into a deep recess.

Martens parks the car in the last stall before the cinderblock wall marking a dead end. As they idle, Arnason watches the entrance to the alley for the dealer they're meeting, some kid a few years out of high school with expensive taste in streetwear and an attitude to match. Normally they play classic rock or the alt-music station, but right now the radio is tuned to the news. One of Arnason's great fears is that one day he will hear one of the deep-voiced men or even-keeled women call his name, not for some act of bravery in the line of duty or for busting open a case that puts his small community at ease, but something else, something from this aspect of his life that he wishes so much to keep hidden until his body is dust.

Before long, a tall kid wearing joggers and a hood rounds the corner with his head down. He approaches the car and taps on the back window. Martens unlocks the car and the kid gets in the backseat.

What's good, boys, he says, taking off his hood.

Business as usual, Martens says. We've got your resupply.

Dope, the kid says. It's been mad busy all week. This shit is moving, man.

Arnason pulls a black plastic shopping bag from beneath his seat and passes it back. The kid takes it, opens it up, and peers inside. Fuck, dude, he says. This is like half of what I can dish tonight at the grounds.

Yeah, well, Arnason says. We've got priorities this weekend.

I've been selling for you for two years now and you're saying I'm not your fucking priority?

Arnason unbuckles his seatbelt and turns to face the kid directly. That's right, he says. You're not.

That's bullshit, man.

We've got a lot of mouths to feed, says Martens. He looks at him through the rearview mirror. You'll be back on track next week.

No fucking way, the kid says. He slams his hand against the headrest of Arnason's seat.

Arnason's head lurches forward with the blow. He feels the pressure of it behind his eyes.

I need that cash now. Let me be your fucking guy.

Arnason closes his eyes. He breathes deep. Then he pulls his gun, turns back, and points it so the kid can see straight down the barrel. You're not my fucking guy, he says.

The kid puts his hands up, presses his body back into the bench seat. Chill, man. Chill.

Arnason cocks the gun. He holds it like that for a moment, one light trigger-press away from discharging. Then he uncocks it and returns it to his holster. Same place, same time. Next Saturday.

The kid nods. His body sinks, sheepish now.

And you better have all the cash, Martens says. We will fuck you, kid.

Arnason glares at his partner.

All of it, the kid says. Of course. Always. You got it. Then he's up and out the door, walking fast down the alley and onto the street.

Martens puts the car into reverse and pulls out of the stall. Mouthy fucking kids, he says. Two more drops, right?

That's it, Arnason says.

I can't believe you pulled your firearm on that kid. You're sketchy as hell today.

Arnason doesn't reply.

If you get us into any shit, I will sell you out. You know that, right?

Arnason runs his hand through his hair, grabbing it in a bunch at the back of his head.

I'm joking, man, Martens says. Just jokes.

Arnason breathes in through his nose and out through his mouth, in through his nose, out through his mouth. His revolver weighs against his hip. Each time he points his weapon at another person, he can feel his grip on whatever it is that makes him human loosen just a little bit, like a rope that slips through your fist, only an inch or so at a time, and you don't have any way of knowing how far you've got until the end.

DALLAN DERMOTT

He takes another gulp of his beer, conscious of the heat building in his cheeks and the lightness in his head. The energy in the room is like a fine mesh electric fence caging him inside himself. He has difficulty taking anything in or getting anything out. He manages to blurt a short and muddled sentence from behind his teeth. There's no way I'm taking those pills, he says.

Are you kidding? Hannah says. Of course not. Not tonight, not with what happened to your friend.

Brooks, he says. You can say his name.

You're right. Brooks.

If your brother tries to get us to do it, just pretend to put it in your mouth and then slip it into your pocket or whatever.

Right, Hannah says. I used to do that with the multivitamins my mom forced me to take as a kid. They were like horse pills.

Dallan gets up. I'm going to go find the bathroom. He shuffles out from between the coffee table and the couch and moves to the hallway at the far end of the living room. It's not a big apartment, but he asks someone where the bathroom is, just to be sure. He's directed to the other end of the hall, a closed door on the far wall. He doesn't want to spend any more time alone than he has to in a crowd of Thomas's friends.

He holds his ear to the door but can't tell if it's occupied on the other side, not with the music thumping from the living room. There is a small puddle of light coming from the bottom of the door. When he tries the knob, his weight pressed against the hollow veneer, it turns and he stumbles in.

There is a small group of people inside, four of them. A young woman is on her knees with two men standing above her. She has one of them in her mouth and holds the other close to her face, her hand wrapped around him and moving back and forth. She makes eye contact with Dallan and he can see her eyes watering. There's another man by the counter with his phone out, taking a video of the other three, and he also has his pants part way down, touching himself as he watches the woman and the other men.

Dallan jumps back out, jerks the door shut, and holds his forehead against the cool surface. He needs air. He walks back down the hallway and turns for the kitchen. Hannah is talking with her brother, the two of them side by side on the couch without him there between them to stifle the conversation. She even laughs at something her brother says and it relieves Dallan to see her happy. She deserves a refuge from the position that he's put her in. Dallan shuffles around a circle of people where the carpet meets the linoleum of the kitchen floor and he makes for the balcony door.

A young couple smokes and talks in hushed voices at the far end of the platform and he makes no effort to disturb them. He makes for the opposite end of the balcony, shallow but as wide across as the unit itself, and rests his forearms on the wrought iron railing. He leans over and looks down into the street. The alleyway behind the building is lit by the streetlights in a series of dim yellow pools spaced along the road on alternating sides. He wants to go home, to crawl into bed and wait as long as he can before his parents or college or some other responsibility comes and forces him back into the world. A future beyond his guilt and grief seems impossible right now, in the strange lingering heat of the early evening. Though he knows that future has to exist for him if he's to stay on as a person in the passage of time, ending each day in darkness and rising again to meet the light.

Below him in the concrete yard behind the building, a man comes into his periphery. He walks out along the path on the side of the building and then makes for the chain-link fence and the gate to the alleyway. It's Thomas's hook-up, the guy he pointed out earlier. He unlatches the gate and walks down the alley, where he stops at a car, an older brown sedan with squared features instead of the more rounded contemporary look. It's parked in front of a garage with a retractable door covered in moss, its roof sloping in from years of rain and neglect.

A man gets out from the passenger side and walks around to the trunk. He steps into a beam of light from an incandescent lamp above and Dallan immediately recognizes him. It's the officer again, in the heavy leather jacket. Even in the early evening, he must be sweltering beneath it. He lifts the trunk and digs around. He removes a black plastic bag and hands it over to Thomas's friend, who turns without a word and walks back towards the apartment. Dallan watches the young man, his quick and measured steps, and when he goes to look back at the car, the officer is staring back in his direction. Can he see him from this far away, make out his features? It's dark on the balcony. Dallan is backlit by the sliding glass door, probably nondescript, and there's a good distance between them. The longer the cop at the car stares, though, the more nervous Dallan becomes. The man slams the trunk closed, holds his gaze a moment longer, and then gets back into the car. A bout of blue smoke puffs from the exhaust and it drives off.

Dallan can feel a panic building in his chest. He makes for the door and stumbles through the kitchen back to the couch, where

Thomas and Hannah are still talking. As he is bending down to get her attention, he sees the dealer come back in through the front door of the apartment and head straight for the three of them.

Hannah acknowledges Dallan, and though she is smiling at first, her face hardens with concern when she sees his wide-eyed anxiety. Before either of them can say anything, the dealer plops down onto the couch and throws his arm around Thomas.

He waves a small opaque grocery bag beneath Thomas's nose, white teeth grinning like a cat presenting a fresh kill to its owner. Who wants in on this? he says.

Thomas grasps his hand on his shoulder and kisses him on the cheek. You're a fine sunnoabitch, he says.

How much you want?

I need two hits for myself, Thomas says. He turns to Hannah for confirmation. And another couple for my sister and her friend here.

Thomas's friend opens the bag and peers in, ruffles around with one hand until he's found what he's looking for. He pulls out two small ziplocks, each with two small white tablets, smaller circles pressed into their centres. He passes one to Thomas and then reaches over him to offer the other baggy to Hannah. You sure this is all you want?

First time, she says.

This isn't much, he says. You'll want more later on if you start rolling now.

Don't pressure my little sister, Thomas says. You cheeky prick. He opens his wallet and shoves a couple bills into his friend's hand. If she wants more, we'll come find you later on, okay?

Sure, he says. Sure, just shoot me a line.

He leaves them be. Dallan watches him stop in on one group after another, distributing the contents of his bag and taking palmfuls of cash in return.

Let's make a toast, Thomas says. He pours one of his pills into the palm of his hand and waits for Hannah to do the same.

Right now? Dallan asks.

Fuck yeah, Thomas says. Why wait?

Let's do it, Hannah says. She opens the baggy and drops one into her hand. She turns back to Dallan and offers the bag to him.

He accepts it and tips the final tablet out. Without hesitating, he shoves his hand over his mouth, holding the pill outside of his mouth against the dry skin of his bottom lip, and quickly pulls it away. The chalky tablet is stuck to his palm and he slips his hand into his pocket to get rid of it. With his free hand, he takes up his beer and pretends to wash it down.

Thomas follows him, dry-swallowing with a sharp rise and fall of his Adam's apple. He looks to Hannah next and says, Let me see that pill in your mouth.

What? she asks, her fist still clasped in her lap.

It's a tradition of mine, he says. I like to see my friends take them for the first time. I call it The Contract. You're *bound* to have fun.

Hannah shakes her head. What about him? she says, gesturing to Dallan.

The narc went too fast. At least we can do it proper for you.

She turns her body to her brother and brings her fist to her mouth. Dallan is leaning all the way forward, practically off of the couch to watch her. She opens her mouth. The pill is resting on her tongue and she shows it to Thomas and then Dallan. She closes her mouth, takes her beer, and tilts her head back, swallowing. After she's done, she opens her mouth again. Empty.

DEPUTY ARNASON

As he approaches the station, he's on edge. He opens the heavy glass door and walks through the reception area. He doesn't stop to say hello or make small talk with the clerk at the counter and he can see her eye him as he cuts through the room, all quiet except for his footsteps that echo off the ceramic tiles of the floor and the white walls, bare except for the posters promoting various community safety initiatives. He goes into the back, past the interrogation rooms, and weaves his way through the cubicles, mostly empty on a Saturday night. Only a portion of the fluorescent ceiling lights are on and the room is bathed in a half-light, the rolling chairs and lamps casting odd shadows across the grey-blue carpet.

He stops at Sheriff Durham's door and takes a deep breath. The blinds are closed, but the sepia tone of his brass desk lamp leaks through the cracks. He knocks.

Not now, Durham calls from inside.

It's Arnason.

There's silence.

Arnason, sir, he says again.

If you're not going to fuck off then I guess you better come in.

He opens the door and is hit with the smell of smouldering pine from Durham's incense, the white smoke of it curling and snaking in the space before the sheriff. He is leaning back in his leather office chair. A wad of chewing tobacco forces his bottom lip out in a pout.

Shut the door, Durham says.

Arnason does so, takes a seat opposite his boss.

How'd it go at Red Pheasant?

Fine, Arnason says. He folds his arms.

Good, Durham says. He spits into his white ceramic mug. And the deliveries?

We made a few drops to the usuals. Stopped off in a laneway on the east side to make the last one.

Sounds uneventful.

Arnason swallows, sits up straight in his chair. I saw that kid again.

What kid?

The kid from earlier today.

You'll have to be more specific. I've received a lot of reports about a lot of kids. It's the weekend for that sort of thing. Every year they try to burn it all down, the little shits.

The one who was here, in room four. He knew about the carnie.

Oh yeah? You see him at Sunsetter chucking his cookies on the Gravitron?

I saw him when we were making the delivery at that east-side laneway.

Durham runs a finger between his teeth and bottom lip, scooping out the wet brown ball of tobacco. I've been chewing this shit for twenty-five years and I still can't pack a tight dip. He flicks the wad of tobacco off into the mug, brings it to his lips, swishes saliva around in his mouth, and horks another ball of spit. So you saw him while you were making your runs?

Yes sir.

And you're sure it was him?

One hundred percent. It was him.

I assume you're telling me this because it's somehow important to me. So what happened?

I just saw him there on the balcony of that apartment building. I stared him down, real hard. It was definitely him.

We've fucking established that, Durham says. Did he see you?

It was dark, but I think he saw me.

So then what?

What?

What did you do after this kid saw you?

I didn't do anything. I got in the car with Martens and we took off.

You didn't go up there and knock on the door? Bust the party up? Have a word with him?

I didn't.

Durham clears his throat. We can't have this. Not right now. We need a goddamn seamless operation this weekend.

You don't think I know that?

I'm having real trouble understanding you these days, what you are and aren't aware of. Durham stands now, hikes his pants and straightens his collared shirt. But this is a problem, a big one, this kid going around out there, knowing what he knows—

—we don't know what he knows.

Don't piss on my back and tell me it's raining, Arnason. He's going to talk eventually. He's at that age when they'll say anything to anyone. They'll run their mouths. They're not afraid of us. They have no sense of consequence, no shame. He bends low and puts his hands on the desk. This is on you. I don't have to remind you what happens if our involvement in all this is dragged out into the light.

I'm well aware.

So what are you going to do about it?

I guess that's why I'm here.

You've got a proposal?

I think we can find the kid tonight. That party he was at, they're almost definitely heading to the grounds later. I think we can rough him up a bit, intimidate him, scare him a little.

Scare him? Durham repeats. No. He picks up a paper from his desk, crumples it into a ball, and tosses it at the trash can in the corner. It hits the rim and falls to the floor. That doesn't change the fact that he's seen you. He knows your face, what you do—and both lines of work, too.

The pit in Arnason's stomach rises to his throat. He tries to swallow it back down. That's all I'll do, he says.

You know what we've got going on here? You know what happens to you if this gets out?

Arnason is losing his patience. I told you. I'm aware.

There's a shitstorm coming for you if you don't make this right. If it's not some hotshot prosecutor, it'll be muscle from our friends up north. You might end up food for the weeds at Red Pheasant.

Arnason looks Durham over. He's known him for so long, but never has he seen his face in such a foul frame, the sinister creases of it, the deep wrinkles that betray the wickedness constantly simmering just beneath. He does not blink. He does not look away.

What are you going to do about your mother while you're locked up? Is your wife going to change her diapers while you're doing fifteen in high security? Or just plain old fucking dead?

A burning rises in Arnason's chest. He can't swallow it back down. He stands and glares down at Durham, biting his lip. The smoke from the incense sears the back of his nose and makes his eyes water. He wipes his face and holds himself over Durham for as long as the tension in his body can keep him there. Then he storms through the door and slams it behind him.

It's not the first time Durham has pushed Arnason in the direction of a line he would rather not have to cross.

He's been distributing drugs to various dealers and footmen around town from the first day he accepted Durham's offer to get in on the side hustle. Two months in, the sheriff gave Arnason what he considered at the time to be a test. One dealer, a cocky kid around nineteen or twenty, had become a liability to Durham and his suppliers up north. It started out with him mouthing off at parties after a few too many, dropping hints about who he got his product from and maybe even where they got it themselves. Arnason was in charge of his re-ups and when he came up short three weeks in a row, it was decided that he was either dipping into his own supply or skimming some off his revenue. Arnason brought this to Durham's attention and he was given the order, passed down from the supplier. The only people who hated sticky fingers more than Durham were the guys up north.

Arnason picked the kid up on his normal Thursday night delivery, but told him he needed some muscle for another drop off to a dealer who'd been giving him trouble. He knew the kid's type, that if he played to his ego, his sense of masculinity, he could get him to go anywhere, do anything for him.

What Arnason did was drive the highway north that he normally took to make pickups at Red Pheasant, but on that night he kept driving, under the overpass, past the course, and further on into the sparse fields and pastures that stretched sometimes for hours without interruption between the towns and cities of the region.

Where is this job anyway? the kid asked him.

Just outside the next town, fifteen minutes maybe, thirty at most, is what Arnason said.

They drove until it was dark and then Arnason turned onto the range road he had picked out earlier that day as he studied a map for the most remote nature reserve he could find within a reasonable distance. It was a bog famous for the rare plains bison that roamed its woods and clearings, frequented only by birders or school groups who kept to the boardwalk paths to avoid sinking knee deep in the sponge-like ground. He remembered visiting this place when he himself was in school and was told how the first colonizers used to burn the dried patties of bison shit in a pinch to keep warm during the harsh winters.

Arnason pulled over on the shoulder of the dirt road and told the kid to get out. From the trunk he removed two pairs of rubber boots, one for himself and one for the kid, and a large black Maglite.

The guy we're looking for, Arnason said, he lives in a cabin through these trees here. We're going to surprise him from the back.

The kid nodded, cracked his knuckles as if he were heading for a fight, and Arnason led them through the brush and muck until they came upon a meadow. There was a pond at the far end of the clearing and on its surface were large lily pads, round black shapes on the midnight blue of the water. They were far enough from town that the sky was unpolluted by its light and Arnason looked up and saw all the same stars he used to see when he went camping as a boy. Bullfrogs all around them, hundreds of them it must've been, croaked from the darkness.

That was where Arnason turned to the young man who was following him and pulled his pistol. He pointed it at the young man and they stood together, both of them shocked and still in the meadow, and heard the bullfrogs and smelled the musk of the rich, damp ground that surrounded the pond.

Get on your knees, Arnason told the kid. Kneel.

When he didn't kneel, Arnason smashed him in the mouth with the butt of the Maglite. He shined it again on the kid and saw his mouth gushing with blood, his front teeth, top and bottom, knocked in.

He got on his knees. His face was twisted and snot trailed from his flared nostrils and bloody spit dripped from his bottom lip as he mouthed something over and over again to Arnason, something he couldn't quite make out as the breeze whipped up the leaves and the branches of the trees above them, and the frogs went on.

Arnason approached the young man and pressed the point of his gun to his forehead. The tip of the barrel settled into the taut skin. He cocked the hammer. The boy looked up at him through his tears, one eye staring past each side of the barrel. Arnason remembers the surge he felt then, the power he had over that young man that seemed to tense every muscle in his body, but also the feeling that followed it, the shame and remorse for making a person turn and stretch his face into such a monstrous display of fear, of helplessness.

He stepped back from the kid and, with the gun still pointed at him, told him to go. He told him to run north and keep running all night until he reached the next town. Arnason wouldn't tell a soul where he was. The boy wouldn't get in touch with anybody, not even his own family. He was to catch a train or a bus to a different corner of the country—or another country altogether. He was to go and stay gone, a ghost from now on in the place he grew up, a story locals would recite to each other with no final explanation, no conclusion. He would not be coming back.

In the parking lot outside the police station, Arnason leans against the old brown sedan and remembers that night. He draws deep breaths, trying to cool his insides, but it's no use. He lunges around the front of the car and pukes onto the asphalt. There is no good in any of this. None to come of it, either. He knows this. He wonders when all the good disappeared from his life.

HANNAH FIELDS

Everyone from the party has congregated in the parking lot outside the Amber Arms. Some of them, groups of four or five, are getting into cars and trucks. Some climb into the trunks and have their friends shut them in. Others are smoking and laughing, still sipping from dark bottles of beer. One throws an empty across the parking lot and it shatters on the brick wall of the next building over. Across the road, a figure opens a door and peers out before retreating back inside.

Hannah passes her hand along her forearm. She can feel every hair follicle light up like a small spark as the soft skin of her fingers moves over them. She is happy, she thinks, for the first time since the night before, and probably longer than that. Maybe this happiness is an artificial one, but she can't tell the difference. There was the nervousness, the full-body excitement she felt knowing Nick was back in Perron, but that was not happiness. It was something else. Before that was the emptiness of having Nick so far away, though there were glimpses of happiness in the moments they shared on the phone when he could steal some time to talk. Her mind swerves to thoughts of him like an insect diving at a bulb in the night.

Dallan stands beside her, twisting the soles of his shoes on the rough asphalt. He has his hands in his pockets. How do you feel? he asks.

Amazing.

I know it. He runs his hand over his pocket where she knows the small white tablet is still concealed. I felt like a firework last night.

Why don't you join me?

Dallan cocks his head, confused.

She looks deep into his eyes. Join me.

Are you kidding?

Look at me. I'm fine. I feel good for the first time in forever.

I don't want to die.

You're not going to die.

You can't promise me that.

I promise. She lowers her eyes at him. She doesn't want to be alone in this, wants Dallan close to her in this. She wants to bring him into her sanctuary now and have him share in the feeling of limitlessness. She wants to take away some of that pain that he must feel, the kind she knows all too well.

He takes the pill from his pocket, stares at it in the palm of his hand.

All of this is such shit, she says. After this weekend, nothing is ever going to be the same for either of us. I just want to be fucked up right now.

He looks her over and then stops and holds his gaze on her own.

She can't remember the last time he held eye contact with her. She is trying to make sense of Dallan, his occasional boldness, and how the rest of the time he seems so apprehensive of everything and everyone. She supposes what happened with Brooks has changed him profoundly. She would probably never know what he was really like before that, above or below his surface. And Nick—Dallan had a hand in that, too, though she believes him when he says he never meant for it to happen. It must have rearranged all the small, unseeable parts of Dallan, that combination of molecules and emotions that once made him a person, the kind that was commonplace and ordinary, as she had always known people to be.

DALLAN DERMOTT

He is staring intently at the small white circle in the centre of his palm. Brooks going cold and still in the dark grass, his chest rising and falling and not rising again—it plays in his head, a vicious loop. The fear of that same fate has seized him. He stays that way, stone-like with inaction, until his apprehension is replaced by a bright and blinding excitement building from elsewhere inside of him. It's a half-formed truth that he slowly begins to accept as self-evident: that he is invincible.

He brings his hand to his mouth and reaches out for her beer. She gives it to him and he washes the pill down.

HANNAH FIELDS

They opt to walk to the Sunsetter grounds instead of hitching a ride with Thomas or one of his inebriated friends. The rodeo is only twenty minutes away by foot despite being on the far western edge of town. The river runs north to south, Perron spreading out like a brushstroke along the bottom of the river valley. They skip over downtown, taking the alleys behind the Chinese food restaurant to avoid the lights and noise of the cars driving by, all of it made more intense and piercing by the substance coursing through her veins.

This euphoria—it pushes Hannah to remember her last night with Nick the summer before. In the brief window after the closing of the Sunsetter last May, before Nick had to start helping with the tear down of the various carnival rides, they stole away to the trailer he shared with two other sophomore workers.

Nick opened the door while Hannah waited on the fake turf patio. He called the names of his roommates and when he was sure the trailer was vacant he waved her inside. He locked the door behind her and wedged a chair from the kitchen under the door handle for good measure.

They came together and kissed each other with reckless, unco-ordinated abandon. She clawed at the back of his shirt with the skin on the tips of her fingers, her nails short and innocuous from years of nervous biting. She untucked his shirt from the waist of his jeans while he moved his hands, first with his fingers at the hem of her shirt, then beneath it along the skin of her stomach and over her breasts with his palms.

They stepped as one body backwards to the twin bed at the end of the trailer where she pulled her dress over her shoulders and head and he unbuttoned the fly on his jeans, sitting down on the foot of the mattress and then kicking them off one leg at a time to the floor. She fell onto him with all her weight and he caught her with his forearms and then let her down gently onto his chest. He reached down the sides of her torso to where the band of her underwear clung to her hips and he worked his thumbs beneath the elastic and guided them down past her knees. She twisted and slipped them off her feet and brought herself forward. She rocked on top of him like the arms of the pump jacks that used to move in all the fields surrounding Perron and when she came he came and she fell again onto his chest, her head resting in the crook of his shoulder and neck and her breath against the pillow warming her cheek.

In the streets, empty save for her and Dallan, it's either the drugs or something else that makes her whole body vibrate as if she is there in that trailer again with Nick. She returns to her present and the feeling disappears from her legs and lower belly. She is not sure how long she has been quiet, but Dallan doesn't seem to mind being alone for a moment with the world around him in this state of what must be similar bliss.

They cross the pedestrian bridge, painted a caustic bright red the year before by the Perron's public works department for the annual children's festival, and from there it's only one long road through the new industrial park to the grounds. The buildings are all drab grey or light blue, with loading bays occupied by long-haul semi-trucks, their doors closed for the weekend, locks checked twice and then three times to keep out the drunks and delinquents who might wander past after the Sunsetter shuts down for the night. The trees planted along the boulevards are uniform and uninteresting, nothing like the old growth of the residential neighbourhoods in the heart of town.

I never liked the rodeo, Hannah says, breaking a long silence between them. My parents used to take me every year when I was kid. We'd go see the clown show, the one where he taunts the bull and then hides in the barrel. I thought it was perverted.

Perverted? It's just a clown.

I hate clowns. I cheered for the bull.

Everyone does. I think that's the point.

See? She pokes him in the shoulder. I just don't get it. It makes me feel cruel and I don't want to be cruel.

Do you think that's what I am? Dallan asks, without looking up.

What?

Do you think I'm a cruel person?

She grabs his shoulder now and stops him from walking any further. She turns his body towards hers. Dallan Dermott, she says. You are good.

You think?

You don't have a bad bone in your body, she says. I don't know you that well. But at least I know that. Now come on, she says. She starts walking again and he follows along. Why do you keep coming back to our annual local horror show?

I've gone every year of my entire life. Used to be with my dad to do the regular stuff, ride a couple rides and watch the rodeo. Last couple years it's been mostly to drink beer. Brooks and I would always chug six in the forest and then try to sneak into the gardens to catch the bands. That or we'd sit behind the tent to listen while we smoked. Sometimes we'd try to get folks to boot us a couple beers and pass them out underneath the wall of the tent.

People would actually do that?

They love it, he says. It's just like your brother tonight. There's something exciting, a little dangerous about helping teenagers get messed up, I think. They've all been there before, right?

And I bet you're going to pay it forward one day.

Wouldn't you? Dallan laughs. There's something about being a little fucked up, surrounded by strangers, that's always made things feel okay to me.

You spend a lot of time doing that?

Doing what?

Trying to feel okay?

He laughs again, this time a little quieter, under his breath. He sips at the beer he's carrying, finishes it off, and tosses the can over a fence and onto a stack of four-by-fours piled high in the lumber yard to their left, their ends painted orange and peeking over the barbed wire that spirals along the top length of the chain-link.

As they pause their conversation again and walk alongside each other, she can hear the distant bass pulsating through the dark. They round the corner and, all of a sudden, like a futuristic city rising out of some untouched land, the bright lights blare like so many multicoloured stars shooting and falling and popping in the night sky.

The roadway is lined with parked cars. There is a group of dormant police cruisers on the road by the treeline. She spits in their direction and Dallan follows her example, does the same. They cross to the gravel parking lot and it's filled from end to end with vehicles, many of which won't move again until the following morning when the responsible folks come back, red-eyed and hurting, to pick up their vehicles and bring them home. People are streaming towards the entrance of the grounds for the big night. Saturday at the Sunsetter. A number of small crowds are gathered around the tailgates of trucks, standing around smouldering charcoal grills or hard plastic coolers. The music is now a fuzz of treble and distortion, only the muffled kick of the bass drum and the pop of the snare perforating the wall of sound.

All of the ticket booths are in operation and it doesn't take them long to get through to a window. Hannah covers the ten-dollar admission for both of them, slides the bill through the slot at the bottom of the plexiglass.

The midway is considerably busier than the night before, but the same smells and sounds—the fryer oil and tinny music from the game booths, the barking of the Carlsbad Company workers—fill the air. Hannah can feel the horrible memory of the night before trying to punch its way through the gauze of ecstasy enveloping her mind.

She and Dallan stumble through the crowds. Some faces she can make out, people she recognizes from working at the clinic. Others are schoolmates or just kids she knew growing up around Perron. The Ferris wheel lurches into motion ahead of them. Below is the black-and-yellow awning, what used to be Nick's tent, now occupied by another young man shuffling the metal disks in his hand like playing cards. She stops for a moment, pauses and considers the strange but familiar sight, but the dissonance of her competing emotions makes it impossible for her to focus on it for long.

Dallan puts his hand on her shoulder. Come on, he says. Let's circle back and take in a few of those shitty bands.

She looks at the booth one more time. Let's go on a ride, she says.

Which one?

She spins around, scans the entire midway, and stops on the swinging ship, its brown hull lit along the taffrail by vintage incandescent bulbs. She points to it.

On their way over, Dallan stops at a booth and purchases the tickets. The line for the ship is short enough that they'll be on with the next group. Hannah rolls from her tiptoes to her heels, watching as the ship holds at the highest point in its arc, then comes thundering back through the middle, the breeze tossing her hair across her face. The bow roars as it glides through the air, carried by the rush of the wheels and their bearings, drowning out the rest of the midway.

When it's their turn, they climb up the metal steps and Hannah takes Dallan's hand and guides him to the very back of the ship, where she knows they'll feel the motion of the ride at its peak. An attendant comes and pulls the safety bar down, locks it over their thighs.

The ship lurches into motion, ascends, at first only barely above ground, and then swings to the far side, where it gains in height and speed. Soon they are taking off into the air back first, and Hannah can see straight down to the ground and through the ride's floor to all the wheels and gears and axles and the hints of grass below them. She feels the movement in every part of her body, a sensation of lightness and electric joy filling her stomach as the ship crests up and into some kind of heaven before dipping back down to earth.

The boat slows and comes to a stop. Hannah and Dallan step away from the ride and they are all teeth, all energy and air. They turn around and head for the large white tents at the far boundary of the grounds. There is a line of urinals beside the beer gardens and people are collected in a mass, waiting for their turn. There is a bouncer sitting on a stool at the entrance to the tent. He shines his penlight on identification cards as people swarm past him into the darkness and the sound.

You got I.D. on you? Dallan asks.

She pats the pockets of her jeans, shakes her head. I left my purse at Thomas's.

There's a way Brooks and I used to sneak in, he says. He takes her by the hand. She can feel the heat of his palm climbing from her fingers to her wrist as he leads her to the side of the enclosure opposite of the urinal area. They come around the side and he stops, gestures towards the security tent.

Best place to sneak in is right under their noses, he says. He points to an opening in the tent behind security, an entrance for the officers to get in and out of the beer gardens quickly in case any fights or other disturbances start up. We need to wait for some kind of distraction to start and then we can follow them right in. They'll be too busy to notice.

How long does that usually take?

Not long, he says. There are more than enough people here looking for a fight. He turns to grin at her, but the smile immediately disappears from his face. He is looking past her. His pupils are dilated, big and black.

DALLAN DERMOTT

It's like the ghost of his friend has been conjured up in the distance from the thrash and exhaust and filtered light of the midway. A near-image of Brooks looks back at him from down the main drag. People pass between them and each time Dallan expects him to have disappeared behind the obstruction. Instead, he remains as real as anything else in this dreamscape. He moves towards Dallan and Hannah until he is only steps away.

Dallan knows his name. He calls out to him. Aaron.

Aaron breaks into tears and collapses against Dallan's body. He wraps his arms around him and sobs into his chest. He joins Brooks's younger brother and weeps for what feels like the first time in his life, a barrier breaking between his grief and the world that's inspired it.

I'm sorry, he says to Aaron. He holds him as tightly as he has ever held anyone. I couldn't help him. He can feel Aaron's jaw clenched against his chest through the fabric of his shirt. He breathes the boy in. He smells just like Brooks.

Aaron pulls back from Dallan's body and looks up at him. He is smaller, slighter than Brooks, but his face tells of the closeness between the brothers. His eyes are the same deep hazel, his hair longer but still defined by the same coarse dark curls. The beautiful jaw giving way to a round and disarming kindness.

Was he alone? Aaron asks.

Dallan shakes his head. He draws in deeply through his nose to catch the moisture collecting on his upper lip.

Aaron mutters something through his contorted frown. He nods.

I'll do anything, Dallan says. Anything you need. Ever.

Aaron falls into him again. He beats his fist against Dallan's hollow back.

Dallan wipes his nose and looks out into the midway beyond them. He scans the crowd until his eyes fall on a sight that stops his breath all over again. It's the cop from the party and his partner from the golf course before. His body sinks. Adrenaline sets in.

Go home, Aaron, he says. He dries his eyes with the front of his shirt. Go be with Bridge. She needs you right now.

The young man nods. Alright, he says. I can do that.

Dallan holds Aaron's shoulders. In a single last look, he strives to convey the love he has for him, greater now that some can be spared in the absence of his brother.

HANNAH FIELDS

As she watches Dallan and the boy come apart, she feels for the first time that she understands what her companion has at stake. The emotion in their interaction, however brief, was so palpable, it's like she has been observing them on some physical plane separate from hers.

Now Dallan stands in front of her, real again, alone and focused on something in the chaotic distance. She tries to follow his line of sight until she hones in on two men, their familiarity unmistakeable.

It's them, he says.

But we're fine, right? They don't know what we look like, she says. They don't know we saw them.

Dallan shakes his head. They were at your brother's.

Where?

Out back. He's the one who re-upped Thomas's dealer.

Hannah watches the two officers draw nearer through the midway.

I meant to tell you, he says. But I don't know what happened. Thomas started up with his shit and the guy gave us these fucking drugs and I got distracted. I forgot.

Did he see you?

I'm thinking now he did.

The cops are close enough to make out and their eyes are trained expressly on the two of them. They break into a rapid walk and the one that leads has a scowl on his face that fills Hannah with dread. In some strange impulse or instinct, she feels her face twist to mirror his.

Dallan grips her hand. Look, he says.

The guards from the security tent are hustling into the beer gardens.

Let's split up. They know me better. They'll be looking for me. You go in through the opening there and if they follow you, you can lose them in the crowd. I'll go the other way, head for the trailers on the other end of the grounds. I don't think they'll look for us there.

Alright, she says. Her heart is pounding and she can hardly catch her breath. Okay.

Meet me there in twenty minutes, he says. He puts his hand on the small of her back and walks her to the entrance behind the security tent.

The trailers on the western edge, okay?

He ushers her in and she turns just long enough to see him sprint off into the wild furor of the Sunsetter before the canvas flap folds closed.

DEPUTY ARNASON

The two kids split up, but the boy is the one he wants, sprinting off towards the corral and grandstand at a pace reserved for younger people. When he checks back for the girl, she is nowhere to be seen.

I'm not up for running, Arnason says. I fucking hate running.

If Durham finds out you saw the kid and didn't get him, Martens says, he'll have your ass.

Yeah? How's he going to find out?

The other officer shakes his head.

Look, Arnason says. You chase the guy, see if you can get him in cuffs, and I'll go grab the girl. She's got to be in the beer tent there. If we have his girlfriend, we can make him come to us.

The two of them head off in separate directions. Arnason goes for the security entrance to the beer gardens. He flashes his badge to one of the guards as they make their way out of the tent with two drunks in cuffs.

Inside is all sound, scalding show lights cutting through the crowd in beams from the stage scaffolding. The tent is packed from wall to wall with people in plaid and denim, hundreds of them in the gymnasium-sized pavilion. A choreographed line dance breaks out in the centre of the room and all movement blends together. He pauses at the edge of the crowd and scans the tops of heads for the girl, any sign of someone going against the flow of the crowd, the swaying of bodies back and forth.

The band starts right up with another song and the guitars scream through the double-stacked speaker cabinets on either side of the stage. There is a monitor directly to Arnason's left and he squishes his face, slaps a hand over his ear. He turns back to the mass of bodies and that's when he sees her. She's stopped on the far side of the tent, watching him. They make eye contact and she immediately turns away and takes off. He charges through the crowd, pushing his elbows into backs and stomachs to clear a path for himself. People cuss him out. Beer spills on his forearms and his shoes. Everything is thick with smoke and sweat and boozy breath.

When he finally makes it to the other side, the girl is gone. He puts his hands on his thighs, bends over. He is out of breath, his chest heaving brief huffs of hot air. But he picks himself up and jogs to the exit. He steps out into the fresh night. It cools the sweat on his forehead. He scans his surroundings, the toilet lines and the queue of people waiting to get into the beer gardens. At the end of the main drag, he catches sight of the girl as she slips between two game booths and away from the crowd.

He can't be bothered to run anymore. There's a large part of him that gnaws and slows him down, with no desire to apprehend either of these two kids. He paces over the dirt and trampled grass, past the corndog and mini doughnut stands, the Zipper ride with its caged cockpits tumbling in wild circles up and down a column of light. Young men and women, drunk or high, stumble past him, brush his shoulders. He catches his breath, concentrates on slowing.

For some time now he has lived in denial of the weight of his work, the consequences of his operations with Durham and the other co-conspirators at the station. For so long he has approached it with a mechanical detachment. He picks up the product, moves it around town. It's simple labour, easy money. But what he's most recently been tasked with, the job Durham wants him to do, it will bring him as far as he has ever come away from the kind of person he initially set out to be, a place he had avoided narrowly in the wildlife preserve with that boy on his knees on the boggy peat. He has never sought the moral high ground, has always been content to get by through greyish channels, still mindful of the obscurity in his periphery. This, he thinks, must be the darkness at the edge of those channels, and he fears he will place his first foot firmly into it if he follows this young woman past the tents at the end of the midway.

HANNAH FIELDS

S he cuts between two walls of canvas and finds herself in the unadulterated night beyond the thoroughfare. There is a diesel generator rumbling, thick yellow extension cords flowing out of it like streaks of canola petals collected in a rut, and a rusted white work truck, dormant, with its tailgate backed against the tent on her right. She looks around and confirms the feeling that she is alone. The trailers are down a dirt path. She can see the dim light from their patio lanterns, the glow from within their murky windows.

She wanders past trailer after trailer, her head on a swivel, looking for Dallan. Some are fifth wheels hoisted up on the beds of pickup trucks, others are tent trailers that you crank up and out of a low box, and there are also larger units, full RVs, like the one her grandparents used to take south to the desert to snowbird the winter away. She does not want to bring attention to herself, so she keeps from calling out Dallan's name, stays on the shoulder of the sparsely lit gravel roadway. She hears people laughing and talking loudly from inside a trailer and moves on down the row.

As she nears the end of the road, she hears her name whispered from her left. Dallan's head peeks out from behind a trailer. He waves her over.

They both crouch down, concealed. She leans her weight into his, if only to feel some part of him against her body.

Did you lose him? he asks.

He saw me in the beer gardens, but I think he got caught up in the crowd. I didn't turn back after I got out. I went out the front exit and came straight here. You?

He was too slow. I don't even think he wanted to catch me. Dallan almost laughs, but catches on his laboured breathing. As soon as I took off behind the rides, he was gone.

What do we do now?

I think we've gotta get out of here. He places his hands over his face and runs them over the side of his head, stretching the skin back from the outer corners of his eyes. Fuck, I can't think straight. But it's not safe here. He pauses again. Let's go for the forest on the north end of the grounds and take the trails until we come out onto the road. I'll walk you home. We can meet in the morning and talk then.

Are we safe anywhere, though?

Better home than here.

She grits her teeth. She wants so badly to rest in her body.

I'll go check if the coast is clear. Then we'll run to the other side and cut across the field to the woods.

He grabs her hand and her skin comes alive, burns and shudders. He lets go and she can still feel the connection like a glow within the clouds when lightning strikes. She looks down at her hands and they seem ethereal, electrified.

Dallan lunges to the front of the trailer, still crouched down as low as he can go without losing his balance. He leans around the corner to look out, but immediately pulls his head back in. He shuffles back to her, quick. Shit-shit-shit.

What?

That fucking cop. He's coming down the road. I think he saw me.

They walk as fast as they can without kicking up gravel or making too much noise into the sprawl behind the row of trailers. There are trucks parked haphazardly, wooden crates for carrying gear, lawn chairs set around folding resin tables where the workers probably take their breaks, but all of them are gone to the midway for their last shift of the weekend.

Dallan points to a truck, the one furthest from the trailers. You go over there, get down behind it. Don't come out until you know it's clear.

Where will you go?

He looks around. Don't worry about me. I'll find somewhere.

She takes him at his word. Without looking back, she sprints for the truck. She swings herself around the side and gets down on her knees behind the rear wheel-well. She can feel the ground, cool and rough, through the denim of her jeans. She leans forward to check for Dallan, sees him open the door to a portable toilet and close himself in. She scans the area but doesn't register anyone else yet. She hunches over to catch her breath.

She is tired of hiding, of running. Maybe she is emboldened by the drugs, but it takes all her willpower not to stand up and walk out and meet the cop head on, tell him that they know what he is and what he does.

When she peers around from behind the truck again, the cop comes from between the two trailers. He is alone. He has a long black flashlight and shines it around at the ground, up into the cabs of the trucks and over the open crates. She grips the rim of the tire, holds herself back.

After inspecting the area for a minute or so, the cop walks up to the portable toilet. He tries the door, but Dallan has locked it. The man knocks. No answer. He tries the door again and then Hannah sees him remove his gun from his holster. He kicks the door hard with the heel of his boot.

DALLAN DERMOTT

The blows to the door explode into the confined space like the inside of a bass drum, the entire plastic structure shuddering with each indignant strike.

In the portable toilet stall, the distant lights of the trailers and midway filter through the opaque roof, casting a dull luminescence on his skin. A small sliver illuminates a spent syringe on the floor beside him. He cranes his neck to change his vantage point. There are bunches of soiled paper, a small broken vial, and a loose orange needle cap.

He alternates his quick, shallow breaths through his nose and mouth. He closes the lid of the toilet to try and contain the pressurized smell of the shit and piss and vomit, the chemicals poured on top to mask it all. He sits down. His skin seethes. All day the beating sun has been heating the air inside the stall to a point so violent it feels as though it is pressing against him from all sides, like it has formed a layer that closes in on all the exposed surfaces of his skin.

Again, the flimsy door booms, three times, and the world around him shakes.

He holds his breath. His eyes are only semi-adjusted to the dark. He squints and makes out the latch that he locked when he entered. He watches as it breaks and the blinding white of a single flashlight pours into the toilet stall. There is a figure, a silhouette behind it. He shields his eyes.

HANNAH FIELDS

The man stands for a moment at the caved-in door, then raises his gun and fires a shot into the small enclosure. The blasts make her whole body jolt. The flare from the barrel of the pistol punctures the dark of the night. He fires again.

Her mind goes blank. The world around her converges into a singular impression, surreal and indistinguishable. She gets up, runs as fast as she can towards the parking lot and the street, through the crowd of people. She can't make out their faces through her tears. The blue-white floodlights streak in her periphery, swirl with dashes of colour from the amusement rides. She doesn't stop to turn around, to see if the man is following her. She is instinct and flight.

All the rasped voices mix with the country music playing from a hundred tinny speakers all around the rodeo grounds. Beneath all of it is the dull thump of the bass from the band. She feels it as a second heart racing in her chest. It matches every second step she takes, drives her on.

The crowd thins in the open space at the end of the main stretch before it collects once more as a mass of people teeming around the beer garden tent. Everyone represents a new danger to her. No one is above the violence she has just seen. She puts her elbows up and pushes through them, the sweat of strangers clinging to her bare arms and face. The air is hot and stale. She can see the exit to the parking lot, the aluminum roofs of the ticket booths beyond the people. She drops her head and makes one final charge to the end of the madness, out into the cool emptiness beyond.

She stops to catch her breath, her arms crossed over her chest. She is sobbing. She wipes her eyes and grabs at her face. She takes a chance and turns back now, but no one emerges from the crowd to follow her. Ahead, she sees her brother and a small circle of people are smoking against the chain-link fence. She goes to him.

Thomas, she says between breaths.

Jesus, he says. You look like shit. You're all red and blotchy, all over your face and neck.

She heaves, gulps at the air.

Are you okay? His friends have stopped talking and now look at her with equal concern.

Your keys, she says.

What?

Give me your keys, Thomas.

Thomas is jolted by the firmness and volume of her voice. He stands up straight. You're fucking high, he says. I'm not letting you drive my truck.

No, she says. She bends over, places her hands on the tops of her knees, her lungs pulling in the outside world like an animal, near-dead from thirst, finally at the pool's edge. I need them, Thomas. You don't understand.

Don't understand what?

I can drive. I promise. But I have to go. I *need* to go. She stands up straight, pleads with him through the moisture clouding her eyes.

He considers her for a moment. Okay, he says. He fishes in both of his jeans pockets until he produces a ring of keys. Where's that narc kid you were with? He withholds the keys, but only briefly. Whatever, he says. Just be careful.

She snatches the ring of keys from him and clutches it in her fist. She checks behind her one last time and when she is sure the cop isn't on her tail, she jogs for the parking lot. She passes between the ticket booths, patronless and quiet now that everyone is already inside the rodeo grounds, and marches down the columns of parked cars, pressing the panic button on the keychain remote, waiting for one of the small trucks to light up and announce itself. The midway fades behind her. The crush of gravel beneath her feet becomes her soundtrack, clear and audible with her own laboured breaths.

She covers the entire parking lot without locating Thomas's truck. At the end of the final row, she scans once more for anything that might resemble his small single cab, the dents on both front and rear bumpers from his semi-habitual fender-benders.

She steps off the curb into the street. The traffic has died completely now. It is both too early and too late in the night for anyone to bother with driving. Everyone in town is where they need to be. In the middle of the black asphalt strip, she points the small keychain remote at various trucks parked along the boulevard. Suddenly, one comes alive, front flashers blinking off and on, its horn sounding in a series of steady blasts. She presses the button again to quiet it.

She unlocks the driver's side door and climbs in, fits the key into the ignition and starts the vehicle up. The dials on the dashboard glow and the stereo cuts in mid-song, the volume cranked and the speakers from his second-hand sound system breaking up on the peaks of treble.

The front headlights illuminate a row of idle police cars parked along the far side of the road. She shifts the truck into gear, reverses to give herself more space to maneuver, and then slams her foot onto the gas pedal to pull out. The tires spin and the engine roars. She keeps the accelerator floored and powers across the street, straight for the patrol cars. She rams a car in the centre of the row, crushing the door panelling, glass shattering over the hood of her truck and down onto the asphalt below. She ploughs on through, forcing the car up onto the curb and over the boulevard. The sound of steel bending and breaking fills the cab. The patrol car tips over the crest of the ditch, and with her foot still planted firmly on the gas pedal, she plunges down into the darkness of the impression below.

SUNDAY

DEPUTY ARNASON

He tilts the bottle back, fills his mouth with the last of the rye whiskey. He leaves it in there a while, his tongue and cheeks numb to the hundred-proof singe by now, and then swallows the liquid in one go. It's near morning and the sun's violent rise advances on the stars, the eastern edge of Perron burning like an ancient city sacked by enemy forces.

He is down on the ground, the small of his back in the dirt, the tall unkempt grass at the base of the abandoned grain elevator reaching as high as his armpits. He is drunk and alone and his eyes are open and can't seem to shut. He tried all night to find sleep there on the hard ground where the wheat pool used to fill freight trains bound for cities to the south and east. He curled up and held himself and used his borg-lined jacket as a blanket, but it was no use.

All night, he thought about a case from his first couple months on the job. A boy from the local high school overdosed, bored and alone in his bedroom on a weeknight, and there was nothing anyone could do. Both his mother and father wept while the para-medics wheeled him out of their home. Later that year, when Durham asked if he wanted to get in on his side hustle, he never even made a connection between the two, but now he can see that boy clear as the day they found him, cold and white and covered in vomit, tucked under a thin sheet in his own single bed.

He's so tired and drunk that he can't see much beyond shapes and colours, but in his mind he strains to resist the image of the boy from tonight, crumpled over on the seat of the portable toi-let, the blood running down his smooth face from the hole in his forehead. It trickled in a jagged line like a crack on a windshield. Arnason made that hole, and he'd even made another one before it, right in the boy's gut. It was a terrible way to expire, shot in the stomach, the blood and acid mixing in your chest cavity and eating you up from the inside, and so he thought it would be best to take better aim and finish the job with one to the head. It was the kind thing, the right thing to do.

He called it into Durham back at the station and they sent a few others to clean up the mess. Once they arrived, Arnason got in his car, picked up the bottle at an all-night liquor store, and made his way to the spot he's in now, a favourite of his on nights he can't sleep or needs to kill time on patrol. He has no idea where the girl went after he killed the kid, only that Durham asked for the boy and that's what he got. Arnason won't give him anything more than that—possibly never again would he do a thing for the son of a bitch. Durham could ruin him or kill him, send him to languish behind bars, or even keep him alive with everyone he loves dead all around him, but he would no longer do his work.

In his heart, he's sure Durham won't let him be. The man is more permanent, more persistent than a cancer.

With the whiskey gone, he lobs the empty bottle at the tracks. It smashes on the steel rails and sprinkles the rocks around them with broken glass. It's getting lighter and his wife will be up soon enough—if she even went to sleep at all in his absence. He left his phone at the station earlier and hasn't spoken to anyone in several hours.

He cross-steps up the ditch through the tall cattails and saw-grass to where his car is parked on the shoulder of the road. He stabs at the keyhole and, after a few unsteady tries at it, he gets the door unlocked.

He takes the back streets where he knows his swerving and abrupt stops have the best chance of going unnoticed. He can't get the book for driving drunk—he's the law and untouchable here—but a little discretion can't hurt. Soon he's coming up on Gervais Street and he cuts out of the laneway onto the main road closest to his turnoff. The streets are ghostly and the night air smells of wet concrete, strange as it hasn't rained in days. Everyone is either sleeping off their hangovers or still drinking somewhere. He makes a right and approaches his driveway at a near-crawl, lurching over the curb and up into the open carport built onto the side of the house.

The house is dark and he walks on his toes down the hall into the bathroom. He takes a piss, his stream splitting into two and showering the seat and lid and tank in dark yellow urine. When he is finished, he flushes and wipes down the toilet as best he can with a fistful of paper. He runs the water cold and splashes three handfuls onto his bare face. He runs a towel over his wet skin and through his hair and then brushes his teeth to try to get the liquor off his breath, rinsing with mouthwash at the end.

He turns off the light and goes to the kitchen. He should eat something, a few pickles or a slice of toast, before he goes to bed. Durham will have questions for him in the morning. There's no chance he'll let him sleep the day through. He comes into the dark room and flips the light switch and finds Joanie asleep in a chair at the kitchen table. Her arms are folded in front of her and she's laid her head in the basket of them. But the light wakes her. She raises her head, wipes her mouth. Her eyelids flutter open. What time is it? she asks him.

Go to sleep, he whispers. His voice slurs as his sluggish tongue stalls out between his teeth and the back of his lips. It's nearly morning, he says.

Did you work the Sunsetter all night?

He touches his finger and thumb to the corners of his mouth. Durham's a fucking prick.

You're drunk.

He waves a hand at her dismissively and removes his jacket, hangs it on a hook on the wall.

You could have called. I was waiting for you. I don't know how late I waited. I fell asleep at the table is how tired I got waiting for you.

Long night, he says. He goes to the sink for a glass of water.

She seems to sense his unease and softens. She goes to him, wraps her arms around his waist from behind, and kisses his cheek. Did something happen tonight?

There are things that happen every night.

Honey.

He drinks the full glass down.

You can tell me.

There's not a goddamn person in the world, he says. Then he stops.

She squeezes him tighter. Tell me, she whispers to him. I'm here for you.

He fills his glass one more time and tilts it back.

I love you, she says. Talk to me.

But he does not respond. He holds her small wrist in one hand, his fingers making it all the way around and then some, tucking underneath his thumb. She is repeating those words over and over, *Talk to me. I love you. I love you.* He thinks that maybe he can feel her pulse.

I need to sleep, he says. Then he removes her hands from his waist, brushes her shoulder, and makes his way down the hall to their bed.

HANNAH FIELDS

Her head is pounding as she opens her eyes to a harsh fluores-cent light above her. Her body feels foreign, her muscles tight and twisted with a soreness she's never felt before. She is lying in a bed that isn't her own. To her left is a low table with a white laminate top, clear of any items save for a box of tissues and a glass of water. She reaches for it, fills her dry mouth, a drop dribbling from the corner of her lips and down her chin. On her right is some kind of machine she doesn't recognize and a stainless steel stand like a coat rack with a bag of fluid hanging from it. From the bag is a clear plastic tube and she follows it down until it arrives at the skin on the back of her own right hand. The needle is held there with medical tape and there is a white plastic bracelet fas-tened around her wrist.

The room smells of commercial cleaners. There is a window on the right side of the room that looks out into a hallway, but she can't make out anything beyond it as her eyes adjust to the light, only the half-formed shapes of figures passing by. There are two wooden chairs with upholstered seating below the window, but they both sit empty. She allows her eyes to follow the baseboards to a closed door. Then she peers up from the floor, past the end of the bed, and finds a man sitting, legs crossed, against the far wall.

He smiles at her and shifts in his seat. His front teeth are slightly yellowed. He is clean-shaven with a full head of salt-and-pepper hair. His blue button up shirt is tucked into his trousers and there is a badge hanging from his belt on the front of his waist.

Morning, he says to her. How's the head?

Her forehead clenches and throbs and she raises her hand to the site of the soreness. She feels a fabric bandage wrapped around the circumference of her head, a damp spot on her left temple. She tries to sit up, but pain shoots through her abdomen and her muscles give out.

Don't get up, the man says. He raises his hand to her. You've been in an accident.

Thomas's truck. The row of patrol cars outside the Sunsetter. A mess of sound and sensation, and then the end of the thread of memory.

The doctor says your head came into contact with the steering wheel when you ploughed one of my cruisers into that ditch there. No signs of anything serious, though. He points to the clear tube leading to her wrist. Figured some fluids might do you good.

The man stands and comes around the side of the bed. He takes one of the chairs from below the window and pulls it up close to Hannah.

My name is Sheriff Robert Durham. Maybe you've seen me around town?

She shakes her head.

Not surprising. Good girl like you doesn't get into the kind of trouble that requires the attention of people like me. But you, he points a finger at her. I know who you are. You're Hannah Fields and you wrecked my patrol car.

Her eyes flicker as she tries to make sense of his tone. There is a kindness in his voice, an understanding, but she doesn't buy it. His entire face is a wall of sinister tension. The lines in the skin above his brow are deep and permanent. There is an exaggeration to his facial expressions that makes them seem somehow vapid and insincere.

He grunts. Do you know how much a good patrol car costs? The vehicles like the ones we have run upwards of twenty-six thousand dollars. That's taxpayer money. Do you pay municipal taxes?

She doesn't respond. She feels for the IV needle in her right hand, picks at the tape with the stubby nails. She wants to leave.

I didn't think so, he says. Then he straightens himself in the chair and crosses his legs once more. That police vehicle you hit in your brother's truck is totalled. It's scrap now. And guess what? The doctor tells me he found traces of alcohol in your blood sample—and even a little something else, too. We don't have to talk about that if you don't want to.

Finally, she feels her voice establish itself in the back of her dry throat. What do you want? she says. Her words are hoarse and gravelly.

I was thinking I was going to have to ask the same thing to you, but here I've got you in a bit of a situation. Driving under the influence, malicious destruction of police property. He stops. Correct me if I'm making a stretch here, but it was malicious, wasn't it?

It was an accident, she says. She just wants him to go away. You're right. I was drunk. I was high.

With her confession obtained, he sits back and bares his yellowed teeth. Then he leans towards the bed, inching up onto the edge of his chair. His face relaxes, becomes stern and expressionless. I would like to offer you a deal. I'm going to allow you to leave here and go home and pretend like none of this ever transpired. But what you're going to do for me, you're going to forget about your boyfriend—what's his name, Dermott?

She remembers the thunder and flash from the end of the gun. The white edges of her vision closing in as she ran until it was only the crush of the gravel under her feet that filled her head. As her brow furrows, she winces at another sharp pain from her temple.

Durham goes on. It looks like his best friend's overdose was too much for him to handle. The way it goes is that he confided in you his plan to take his own life with his old man's gun, get away from all that pain. It sounds like you nearly saw him do it while he was sitting on some shitter out back behind the Sunsetter, where nobody would be there to talk him out of it. You were going to help him, but you were too late. Isn't that right? That frustration, that grief, even pushed you to poor judgement when you tried to drive your brother's truck, drunk and high as you were.

It comes to her all at once: whatever it is that she and Dallan have witnessed—it can only be a small portion of a much larger, more sinister machine. It is too big for her to comprehend, but she can sense the danger that she is now in. The sheriff is not who she expected to come and press her on her involvement with Dallan. She thought it would be the cop from that night, a person she naively assumed to be acting on his own. Now she can see that this virus grows from the very top, like ivy cascading down a hillside, each tendril reaching out on its own and choking the life out of the underbrush.

Her head throbs and she grits her teeth. She meets the sheriff's dark eyes head on with her own. She goes to answer him, but the door at the end of the room lurches open. Her parents burst in. A doctor follows closely behind them.

Hannah sees her mother's eyes begin to water as she rushes to her side, crouches down, and places an arm over the blanket resting on her legs. She caresses her and pouts her lips as she inspects Hannah's head wound. Are you in pain?

I'm fine, Hannah says.

Are you concussed? her mother asks. She turns to the doctor at the foot of the bed standing beside Hannah's father. Is she concussed? Did you do a CAT scan? Did you check for contusions?

Your daughter is fine, Mrs. Fields. She passed out from the shock of the accident. She has bruising on her abdomen, a few cuts and knicks here and there, that bump on her head. Maybe a bit of a headache, but no signs of a concussion. It's nothing that won't clear up with a little rest over the next couple weeks.

Then her mother glares at the sheriff. What did he say to you?

Hannah doesn't answer, instead lets Durham answer for himself.

I explained to your daughter what happened last night.

He wouldn't let us see you until he talked to you first.

I gave her a lecture on the dangers of recklessness and negligence is all. We understand accidents, how sometimes external forces can get the better of us. He glances at Hannah. We won't be pressing charges if that's what you're concerned about, Mrs. Fields.

Hannah watches her mother clasp the sheriff's hand and she hates her for it, however fleetingly. He rises from his chair and adjusts his pants with his thumbs tucked in the pockets. He is relatively fit for a man of his age. His stomach protrudes only an inch or so beyond the hem of his waistband.

If you have any additional questions for us, feel free to drop by the station. Just ask for Robert.

He tips his head at her mother, then her father and the doctor, and leaves the room. Hannah watches the door, expecting him to reappear, but after a moment it's clear he's gone.

Can I go now? she asks.

You're ready to be discharged, the doctor responds. You'll need to go straight home and continue to rest. When the shock wears off you might experience some additional pain. I'll write you a prescription for that.

What can we do? her father says.

Is she living with you both?

She is.

Check in with her, ask her some routine questions. What day of the week it is, first and last name, that sort of thing. Just to ensure her cognitive functions are normal. Though again, I haven't seen any signs she's concussed. Rest and pain relief will be the most important part of her recovery for the next few days. Make sure she's comfortable. The doctor turns to Hannah. You can take that bandage off whenever you like.

Her father nods and shakes the doctor's hand. Her mother, the lush, even goes so far as to hug him.

†

In her living room, Hannah stretches out on the couch, several pillows propping up her head. The television plays a property flipping show on silent and unadulterated light pours in through the large bay window.

She has no appetite, no desire to move or be moved. Her parents tried to dote on her when they first returned from the hospital, but after she told them off several times they finally got the message and have not returned in several hours. On her way back from the hospital, she felt the heat of the day, an unnatural flare even for late May. Outside she can tell the whole natural world is thirsting, but inside her home, with the central air humming, it is temperate and stale.

If she is a pool of hurt then anger is the spring at her centre. Nick is gone and now so is Dallan. The life she had been building in her mind, the possibility, the beautiful potential of it, was erased as quickly as her chance at making sense of its disappearance. She wanted justice, closure for Nick, but now there is only this second void. She doesn't know what Dallan was to her, but there was softness there and a brand new chance at living a life beyond the frustration and stagnation of her own. Those frustrations are being reduced to a rage so vital and plain she doesn't recognize it as a part of her.

She wishes she could paint to pass the time, but it bothers her head to focus too long on any one thing. Instead, she lies and stares at the curves and drifts of the brushed plaster ceiling while a man on the television breaks through kitchen cabinetry and drywall with a crowbar and a sledgehammer. She hears her mother moving around in the kitchen, likely fixing lunch for her father and herself. The refrigerator door opens and closes with a palpable, almost awkward gentleness. The cutlery drawer is pulled and then pushed with a measured patience. It's all too much.

Mom, Hannah calls to the kitchen.

She hears her mother's footsteps pitter across the faux-wood laminate floor. She feels her presence approach and soon she is above her, leaning over and smiling. Yes, honey? What do you need?

I need you to go.

What?

I need you to take dad and go somewhere that's not here, not in this house.

We're supposed to be watching you.

I'm fine. Really. I am. But I can hear you tip-toeing around back there and it's infinitely worse than if you were just acting normal. You're being weird, Mom.

I'm not being weird.

You're being so fucking weird.

You're hurt, honey. You were in an accident.

I'm fine. Get Dad, take him to the rodeo or something. Isn't it bull riding finals today?

Always on Sunday.

There. Perfect. It's his favourite. Take him and go. Hannah sits up. Dad, she calls in the loudest voice her pounding head will afford her.

Soon he, too, is tiptoeing into the room like a buck in a glade during open season.

What's wrong, dove?

You're going with Mom to watch the bull riding.

But we're watching you here. We're taking care of you.

Not anymore.

He looks at his wife.

Go on, Hannah says. Get out of here. I just want to be alone right now.

Are you sure?

I *need* to be alone right now.

What about the pain?

It's fine. I'm fine.

Bull riding, he says. It *is* my favourite.

I know, Hannah says. So go.

Maybe we should give her some space, her father says.

Her mother sighs. Do you have your phone?

Yes.

And you'll call us if anything feels wrong? *Anything*.

Yes.

And you have your medication?

Hannah points to the translucent orange pill bottle on the coffee table next to a glass of water.

You need to take two more in forty-five minutes.

I know.

Okay, her mother says.

Okay then, says her father.

Go, Hannah says.

And they do. Her mother and father look at each other and he goes upstairs to gather his wallet and keys from his bedside table, and she goes to the kitchen for her purse, wraps the sandwiches she finished preparing in agonizing near-silence, and then they pull on their shoes and are out the front door. Hannah hears her father's truck start in the driveway, grateful for the distancing of the engine backing out and then taking off down Madonna Drive.

She sits up. Her bruised muscles shudder in protest. She runs her hand over her forehead, over the cut now covered by a large band-aid. It stings, only slightly, as her fingers pass over the place where the skin has split. She goes to the washroom and runs the water in the sink until it flows cold over her hands. She washes and dries them and then fills the small ceramic cup by her toothbrush and sips it, feeling the liquid slip over her tongue and down her throat. It pools in her stomach and cools her from the inside.

In the basement, she goes to her father's gun cabinet. The key is beneath the chess set collecting dust on top of the antique juke-box. Her father has never moved his hiding place, not since she was young, when she used to open the door as a dare to herself when she was alone, never actually touching the contents, only admiring their polished wooden curves and blue-hued steel. She fishes the key from under the dusty marble board, unlocks the glass panelled doors of the wooden cabinet. She passes her eyes over the pair of shotguns, a vintage Remington 870 and her father's Italian-made Benelli, along with his lever-action 30-30 for autumn bucks.

She reaches below the larger arms for her grandfather's revolver, oiled and cleaned meticulously over the years since his passing. She removes it from its place on a velvet cushion and holds it in front of her, feels the metallic weight of it in her hands. At the bottom of the cabinet is a drawer where her father keeps his ammunition. She takes a box of thirty-eight calibre bullets, locks the cabinet, and goes back upstairs.

At the front door, she pulls on her quilted coat and places the revolver in one deep pocket, the box of ammunition in the other.

She drives towards downtown in her mother's car, her arms weak, her hands trembling slightly—even while gripping the wheel at a perfect two and ten o'clock. All around her are the same houses and parkettes and buildings that she has passed nearly every day of her life, the trees whose greens deepen the closer they grow to the river, the dotted yellow line in the centre of the road, chipped and faded since its last reapplication. She sees all of it now in a new and troubling light.

DEPUTY ARNASON

He is hunched over the keyboard in his cubicle. His head is pounding. All over his body, his skin crawls and aches with dehydration. There is a burning in his gut that he tried to exorcise by vomiting in the corner of the parking lot behind the station, but it has followed him in, persisting through the late morning.

The booze allowed him to sleep for four hours straight after he finally found his way into bed, but it was useless—a tortured and toxic rest, his muscles stewing in alcohol, his liver working over-time. He pulls back the head of the vintage drinking bird toy on his desktop, listens to the pendulum click of its beak colliding with the rim of the coffee mug in front of it. For minutes he watches it, the brassy pecks piercing the quiet of the empty office, and then stops it with his hand.

Durham was on his way out when Arnason was on his way in. He imagines the sheriff took one look at his red eyes and pale face, smelled the night before sweating through his skin, and then laughed to himself about it later. Durham told him to stay put until he returned, that they had matters to discuss, but that was several hours ago now. Arnason has hardly been able to stomach a cup of coffee, let alone any food for breakfast, and he is growing more impatient, sicker by the minute.

This Sunday is the hottest he can remember on Sunsetter weekend. By Monday afternoon, he imagines his colleagues will have set up their personal fans inside their cubicles to spin for days at a time until summer has come and passed again. But no such fans are out yet, and nobody has adjusted the central air to match the hot, abrasive air in the building.

Fuck it, he says to no one in particular. He slips his shoes back on, turns off his computer monitor, and heads for the front door.

He walks down the sidewalk with his head down, tired eyes avoiding the sun and bringing into focus only every second or third crack between the slabs of cement. He crosses the street without so much as looking to his right or left. He goes on this way for three blocks until he is at the seniors' care facility.

The weekend administrator buzzes him into the building. At the reception desk, he writes his name into the guest log and heads down the wide hallway to his mother's room. It's quiet for a Sunday. He imagines many of the residents have been checked out by their families and escorted to the Sunsetter grounds for one last bit of the action. That, or the families have gone themselves, seizing the day and foregoing their usual Sunday visits with Grandma or Grandpa.

The door to his mother's unit is closed as usual, so he raps on it three times and then lets himself in. She is in her chair, blinds closed behind her, gumming a Scotch mint or a hard butterscotch candy, looking off at what he thinks is probably not him or anything else in the present physical world, but rather some bit of her jigsawed past that she clings to like a guide rope in a snowstorm.

He sits himself down on the corner of the bed. The mattress is sunken and tired, the springs and cushioning collapsing almost completely beneath his weight. He can feel the hard impression of the bedframe on his backside. He shifts himself into a more stable position on the bed, and then places a single finger on her knee to get her attention. The clouds over her eyes part and she loses whatever vision has been occupying her mind.

Son, she says.

That didn't take long at all today.

What's that?

You recognizing me.

You're my son, she says. I know you when I see you.

He purses his lips at her. Have you looked outside today? It's a scorcher. He reaches behind her and draws the blinds all the way up. The sun spills onto her shoulders and the back of her head, casting her long shadow across the carpeted floor.

She places her hand on her neck as if expecting to grab an actual object causing the sudden heat on her skin. She scratches the back base of her scalp and reaches for another Scotch mint from a rounded crystal container on the top of the dresser beside her. She takes out two and hands one to him.

You look exhausted, she says. What's happened? Aren't you sleeping?

I didn't sleep so good last night.

What's keeping you up? You always slept like the dead.

I don't know. Work's a bitch, I guess.

The only time I've ever seen you not sleep through the night was when you screwed over your friend, Matthew what's-his-name. You took his coin collection and tried to sell it at the pawnshop around the corner from ours.

I was trying to get you roses for Mother's Day. Who knew a dozen roses cost so damn much.

The man at the pawnshop talked you out of selling those coins. Told you they were heirlooms and you should hold on to them. That's a good man, cares about where his money comes from.

That's right, Arnason says. Matt figured it out and his mom called you up that night.

It didn't take much to get you to slide that shoebox out from under your bed and hand them over.

Arnason nods along with his mother's retelling of the story. It's true to the last detail as far as he can remember. Her lucidity today astounds him.

It was the guilt that kept you up, I remember. The shame. You were crying and crying, saying, *I'm sorry, I'm sorry!* You wanted to call that boy every fifteen minutes to apologize again. You were good—I knew it then and I know it now. Look at everything you're giving me. She spreads her arms to the bedroom as if she is the sun and it is her light cast onto the furniture and floor.

Those words sink through Arnason like a stone through still water. He thinks he can feel the acid in his stomach spilling out into his chest cavity, corrupting all that he has left inside that's right and good. I try, he whispers. His eyes sear from the corners outward.

I'm tired, she says. I was just about to lie down for a nap.

Alright, he says.

You should do the same. I can't believe how tired you look. Those bags. You've got to do something about those bags.

Okay, Mom. I'll do that.

Help me up.

He stands and extends his hands out to her, giving her something to pull herself up with. He puts his arm around her shoulder and guides her to the bed.

I need to change, she says.

Do you need any help with that?

Not from you I don't.

Do you want me to send someone on my way out?

I'll manage, she says. If it kills me, I'll manage.

HANNAH FIELDS

S he steadies her phone and, through the window, takes one final picture of the cop with his arm around the old woman, helping her to the bed.

She followed him from the station, left her car parked across Main Street, and watched him as he went down the sidewalk with his head hung low to the old folks' home. Through the glass panel door, she saw him as he stopped at the front desk and then went down the left hallway out of sight. From there, she went around the building from window to window, looking for him on the inside.

She knows the downtown seniors' home as well as she knows any building. Her grandfather lived there before he was transferred to hospice and she explored all the halls and public rooms on her weekly visits when she was younger and her curiosity was at its peak.

On the back side of the building, she found him framed by one of the windows as he opened the blinds and took a seat on a bed opposite of the elderly woman, her grey hair glimmering in the sunlight.

Hannah is crouched behind a manicured English holly in the garden. She must look ridiculous, sneaking around behind the nursing home, but then again there is nobody there to see her. It's the last day of the local obsession and the normally busy weekend visitation spot is empty and tranquil.

When the man leaves the old woman beside her bed and exits the room, Hannah stands and dusts the dry soil from her knees. It is hot and she is sweating beneath her jacket, though she will not take it off, the pockets sagging with the weight of the revolver and the bullets. She pats the fabric, traces her finger down the barrel and over the grooves of the cylinder. She goes back around the building and stops halfway when she sees the cop crossing the street. She walks a little further and pokes her head out, watches him gain distance down the sidewalk, until he turns to enter the police station once more.

She steps out onto the bright sidewalk and makes for her car, sits down on the hot upholstery of the driver's seat and contemplates her next move. She left home without so much as a plan as an innate urge and direction. She knew she wanted to find him and when she did, it dawned on her that she wanted him to know that she had. That's when she took out her phone and started taking pictures. The gun she brought was only a precaution, a threat to levy if and when she found herself face to face with Dallan's killer.

Her shirt sticks to the sweat on her back. She takes a sip from a bottle of water, starts the ignition to run the air conditioning. It blows into her face, stale and tepid, from the vents on the dash. Sure enough, after two minutes or so, an old brown sedan pulls out from behind the station. The cop is at the wheel and he turns out onto Main Street. She puts her car into gear and makes a quick U-turn to follow him.

After a short drive out of downtown, a left-hand turn and then a right onto Gervais, he swerves into a driveway. She trails at a safe distance, four yard-lengths behind his sedan, then pulls over and idles while he exits his vehicle. She puts her car back into gear and rolls up slowly, makes a three-point turn using a driveway across the road, and parks opposite of the house. It is an older neighbourhood, one of the oldest in Perron she thinks, and the bungalows, those that haven't been updated, are covered in weather-stained stucco or faded aluminum siding. His house shows signs of renovation, small efforts that suggest necessity rather than an abundance of pride. Eavestroughs a full shade whiter than the walls beneath them, some patched up concrete on the front steps. The trees on the boulevard are old and knotted. Thick branches stretch out over the street and sidewalk and even onto the front lawns of some properties, threatening to crash through a roof or a window in a bad storm.

There is a large bay window on the front of the house and she can see him through it, taking a seat on the couch in the living room. It looks like he is talking to someone, and eventually a woman emerges from around the corner with a can of Coke in each hand. She sits down beside him.

Hannah takes her phone from her pocket and repeats her ritual, captures several photos of the man and the woman inside together. They face each other on the couch and sip at their cans. He has sunk deep into the cushions and is slouched below her like a coat she took off and tossed absent-mindedly onto the upholstery. Hannah zooms in as far as she can with her device to get a clearer picture. The phone clicks like the shutter of a camera opening and closing. It clicks and clicks and clicks.

DEPUTY ARNASON

When he arrives back at the station after lunch with his wife, Martens is sitting in their shared cubicle and Durham is on top of the desk with his boots on the seat of Arnason's chair. The rest of the office is still empty, everyone either off for the weekend or out on patrol for the final day of the rodeo. Arnason enters the cubicle and hangs his coat on the back of the chair, glares at Durham until he kicks it from under him and into Arnason's shins.

Jesus, Martens says. You look like absolute shit.

Hit it pretty hard last night, Deputy? Durham says.

Arnason slumps into the chair and pedals himself into the far corner where he can see them both without swiveling his aching head.

Martens was telling me how everything went.

Sure, Arnason says.

We got it done, Martens says. His whole demeanour is smug.

You didn't do shit, you rat fuck, Arnason says.

Martens throws his hands up and his brows firm sharply in indignation. You calling me a rat? Seriously? Don't go throwing that word around here, man.

No, Arnason says. He looks at Durham. I should have called you a useless shit stain instead.

Martens shoots up out of his chair and storms over to Arnason. He grabs him by the shirt. I was right there with you the entire time.

Were you? Because I'm pretty sure you were a hundred feet back, bent over, mouth breathing in the midway while I got the job done.

Fuck you, Arnason.

Arnason chops Martens's hand off his collar and pushes him back. And you, he says. He points dead-square at Durham. I did that for you.

Durham grins at Arnason and this sends a bolt of anger through his body so hot he winces.

You tell me, he says to Durham.

Durham lifts his chin at him. Tell you what?

You tell me I did it.

I wasn't there, Deputy. I didn't witness anything. I can't say shit.

You damn well know what I did. You say it. Tell me what I did.

What do you want me to tell you? You want me to say you did your job? You want me to say you killed that kid?

That's right, Arnason says. He is sweating and cold all over. Tell me.

Alright. Durham nods. You killed him. You killed that young man.

I killed him.

You killed him.

Arnason is panting. His fists grip the armrests, his teeth clenched so hard he can't get another word out. He knows hatred now, and it is aimed solely at this man in front of him. The rest of everyone, whatever animosity he has ever felt towards them has been only a fraction of the true feeling. Now he knows: before Durham, it was only shades of dislike, normal human inconvenience. This new feeling is opaque and dark, like looking through a smoked-out window.

You figure out your shit, Durham says. Because this weekend isn't over. We've still got another day of this circus.

Martens is tucked back into his desk chair, his face expressionless, silent.

Durham grabs a file folder stuffed with paper from the desk beside him. And Arnason, he says. Another night, another stack of incident reports. Go down the street and Xerox me two of each. Then you can go home and sleep off your little hangover.

Arnason stands up and gets his coat. Get fucked, he says. Then he snatches the file folder and walks out.

HANNAH FIELDS

At the office supplies store, she goes to the far back corner where the printing services are located. There is an enclosed area with large commercial printers and copiers, various banners and projects on display, a signed poster of a Sting performance framed on the back wall. Several staff members are behind the counter, some of them helping other customers and others labouring over the machines. The acrid smell of ink and hot paper burns her nose.

She needs one of the smaller self-serve printing stations. She approaches one, a small computer monitor in a red box attached to an office-sized Xerox machine. She presses her finger against the touch screen and it lights up. She follows the prompts and plugs her phone, low on battery, into the micro-USB cord beside the keyboard along with a selection of other cords for different devices.

She picks the clearest images from the gallery on her phone, half a dozen of them, and emails them to the address listed on the screen of her ongoing transaction. After a minute or so, she receives a reply email with an order code and she punches it into the self-serve computer. Another half-a-minute and her photos are right there, displayed on the screen.

In the glint of the monitor, she can see someone approach her from behind. The figure is obscured by the ceiling lights reflecting off the screen. Her hands tense into fists, hovering above the keyboard. She whips her head around, but it's only an employee that's come up to her, a middle-aged woman in a red collared shirt and black pants, hair in a tight ponytail.

Can I help you out with anything today? she asks.

Hannah shakes her head, fast and nervous. No, she says. I'm fine. I've got it.

The woman raises an eyebrow at her. You sure? These self-serve things can be a pain sometimes.

Yes, Hannah says.

And the whole email code thing? I hear from people every day about how they get nothing in their inbox after they send their photos in, no product code or nothing, not in their spam or any of those other tricky inboxes, and then they're all freaked out about how their photos are lost in the internet world, being looked at by god knows who, the government or foreign hackers or some smelly teen in his parents' basement looking for kicks online.

Hannah swings her full body around to face the woman. She takes a breath. I'm almost done, she says. I'm all good here.

The woman peeks over Hannah's shoulder to try to get a glimpse of the display, but Hannah steps back to shield it with her body.

I would prefer if you left me alone to finish.

The woman shakes her head. You just let one of us know if you have any trouble, if the printer eats the paper and gets all choked up or whatever.

Hannah nods. The woman leaves her be.

With a renewed sense of urgency, Hannah gets back to work. She completes the order, taps her credit card, and the printer buzzes and whirs. The photos drop out into the collection tray, each with an audible tick. She takes them, warm from the printing process, and slides them into one of the complementary envelopes.

When she turns from the machine again, it's not the store employee she sees, but him. The cop she followed earlier. She freezes. He's here, right in front of her, clear in the harsh industrial lights of the office supplies store.

The cop looms over one of the copy machines along the wall. A stack of paper is wedged beneath the heavy lid of the scanner and he peers intently down at the small screen, his fingers poised above the keypad.

He is confused, she thinks, and she dwells on the idea of a man capable of such an efficient act of killing like she witnessed the night before looking so helpless against this mundane technology. He is just that, after all. A man in a world of men, so resolute in his acts of callousness and violence, now stumbling over something so commonplace, so simple. His hair is greasy and strands of it stick up from a cowlick on the back of his head. There is dirt on the seat of his pants and when he turns his head to look beneath the scanner she can see the dark bags under his eyes. She can almost smell the night on him.

She realizes now there is a place within her reserved for him and him alone. She hates him. It is an uncomplicated hatred, unfettered by empathy or any previous admiration. Will it continue to grow and grow until it rests singularly in her mind, eclipsing all the grief she has been holding and the love that made it possible? She is frightened of it, this emotion unfolding from within her, and wants badly to be free of it.

The cop presses a series of keys on the pad. Below the lid of the copier, the scanner glows. He exhales and stands straight. Then he turns and locks eyes with her. He is still, says nothing. He watches her and she watches him.

Hannah tightens her grip on the envelope of photos and begins to walk as fast as she can without breaking into a full run.

She does not look back. On her way past the display at the end of the final aisle, she snaps up a ten pack of brown paper bags and shoves them into the waistband of her pants.

†

The day has spun on in an unfamiliar ellipsis, at times excruciatingly slow, in other moments unnaturally fast, subject to the shifting gravity of its events. She bides her time in the parking lot of the business supplies store with the radio playing low. A full hour passes, maybe another half. Then she drives back to his house and parks across the street.

She can see him there, lying on the couch now, sleeping or just closing his eyes. The woman who was with him before is still inside. She passes by the window and floats through the room to the kitchen, out of sight.

On the passenger seat, Hannah opens the package of brown paper bags and unfolds one, stands it upright on her lap. She removes the envelope of photos from the bag. It's strange to her, how the woman in the photos appears to her as vibrant and human, but the man seems flat and colourless, as if the world's light doesn't reflect off his skin in the same way. She lays the photos flat at the bottom of the bag. In the glove box, she finds a pen and a sheet of paper. She knows where she wants him to meet her. She tries to distort her letters, hide the identity present in her handwriting, gripping the marker in a fist like a child might do, and writes the location at the top of the paper along with the words *Meet at 6 PM* below.

Then she takes the box of ammunition from her coat pocket and shakes out half a dozen bullets into her hand. She dumps those in, too, and then rolls the opening of the bag closed, running her thumb and finger in a tight pinch over the folds to ensure the flap does not uncoil.

She exits her car, crosses the street, and stands at the foot of the driveway. She watches for the woman to return to view in the

215

front bay window, but after two more minutes, she still hasn't. The man is motionless on the couch. She walks up the brick walkway and then creeps up the front porch stairs. She places the bag in the centre of the porch, turns around, and sprints for the driveway.

She stops when she sees a brick raised slightly out of place where the walkway meets the solid concrete of the drive. She pries at it with the toe of her shoe. It's loose, so she bends down, works her fingers down its side, beneath it, and then pulls it up and out of the earth. The soil beneath it is dark and damp and fragrant despite the heat. A beetle scurries across the patch of exposed soil into the grass beyond. She holds the brick in her hand and tests the weight of it, up and down, up and down.

Hannah goes to the centre of the lawn, cocks her arm back until the brick is just behind her ear, and then hurls it at the windowpane on the top half of the front door. It smashes through the glass. The violent crash jolts her, sends her pulse into a frenzy. Shards spill out onto the porch and into the house. She makes a run for her car.

DEPUTY ARNASON

He is startled, unsure if the shrill sound of shattering glass is dream or reality. His head is raised above the pillow at the end of the couch. His whole body is clenched and his consciousness floats between sleep and something else, the room strange and dark and bright all at once. He rolls his joints to loosen his muscles. The drapes of the bay window are open and the sunlight is cast over his body. He realizes he is covered in sweat. He wipes his forehead with his sleeve and feels the back of his shirt, drenched through.

Joanie stomps around the corner from the kitchen. Christ, she says. What was that?

What was what? he says. He sits up, shakes himself, and remembers the noise that jolted him awake.

Oh my god, she says. She points. The front door. Look at the front door.

In the foyer there is glass spread across the boot mat and floor in shards and smaller slivers. It all glitters there, like a brilliant beach pouring in from the outside.

Joanie walks fast to inspect the damage. There's a brick here, she says. She picks it up and shows it to him. Someone threw a brick through the goddamn window.

He wipes his eyes. I was having the worst dream, he says.

Who cares about your dream? Look at our doorway. She gestures at the wreckage with both of her hands, shaking with anger or shock or both. I'm so fucking tired of your attitude. What do you even *think* about all day?

He cracks his neck and goes over to join her in her reckoning. The brick has scuffed the floor in greyish streaks and a trail of sparkling dust follows behind like the tail of a comet. The large single-pane window on the top half of the front door is now nothing but jagged teeth around a clear opening. He feels a warm draft flowing through it, competing with the air conditioning.

It appears you are correct in your assessment, hon, he says.

What?

That someone put a brick through our door.

Why the hell are you talking like that? Go outside and see if anyone is there.

He tiptoes through the shards, turns the deadbolt, swings the door open, and surveys his front yard and the rest of Gervais Street. Everything is as expected, maybe even a little still for a Sunday afternoon. Then he looks down to the porch, where there is a brown paper bag at his feet.

What's that? his wife asks from behind him.

It's a bag.

What's in it?

I don't know.

Don't open it.

Why not? he says.

It's probably filled with shit.

Dog shit?

It could be human shit.

I'm not afraid of a little shit.

What if it's a chemical agent? she says. Or a bomb?

Bombs don't come in paper bags.

Have you ever seen a bomb? she asks him.

He looks at her with flat eyes, then bends down and picks up the bag. He shakes it. There is some shifting around at the bottom, a metallic rattle sounding from within. He brings it into the living room, the glass still crunching as he steps, less careful now, across the floor of the foyer. His wife follows. He places the bag on the coffee table, front and centre, and then sits down in front of it on the couch where he had just awoken from his dream, the details and sequence of which he still can't recall explicitly but resonate with him as a sense of unease.

His wife is at the threshold of the room. She will not go any further. Her arms are wrapped around her chest and she is shaking her head over and over.

Don't you want to see what's inside? he asks.

She keeps on shaking her head.

He leans forward and grips the sides of the bag with both hands, unrolls the opening with the care of what he imagines an actual bomb technician might employ. He turns it over and dumps the contents out onto the table. A handful of bullets pour out, still in their brass casings. They clink against the lacquered wooden surface, some rolling onto the floor. Then comes a handful of photos, half a dozen or so, glossy and difficult to make out all at once.

Oh my god, says his wife. What are those?

Bullets.

She gasps.

And some pictures.

Of what?

He holds one close to his face and once his brain clicks into focus he can make out the figures in the photo. Of me, by the looks of it.

They're pictures of you?

He brings another one closer for inspection.

And you.

Me?

Some of mom, too.

What the actual fuck, she says. Who took them?

The answer flashes in his mind. It's obvious. That girl at the copy store, she looked at him so intensely, with something he interpreted not just as obsession, but disdain. He did not recognize her at that moment. It was dark the night before, hectic. But he knows now. She's the one he chased through the beer tent at the Sunsetter, who later took off again into the night, right when he fired his second shot. She saw what he did. That young man he killed, he was probably someone close to her, a boyfriend or a brother. He knew how he would look at a man if he killed someone he loved. It would be a lot like the way that girl looked at him.

They're just pictures, he tells his wife. How should I know who took them?

She hurries over to him to see for herself. She grabs one photo, then another and another, and tosses them to the ground. Then she glares at the bullets on the table and down on the carpet.

Someone is trying to kill us, she says.

He holds a picture in his hand. It's of him and his mother, he recognizes, earlier that day. He is sitting down on the bed and she is in her chair by the window. Her grey hair is like a silver creek in the sun. That's beauty, he thinks, his mother in this picture here.

Nobody has tried to kill us yet, he says. But this looks to me like it could be a letter of intent.

He puts the photo down then picks up the small square of white paper. Handwritten on it is an address on the south side of Perron—the middle of nowhere, practically, in the near-abandoned industrial park that used to service the oil industry. *Meet at 6 PM*, it reads.

What does it say?

He folds it and tucks it away in his front pocket. Best you not know for now, he says.

Tell me, she says. You need to tell me what the hell is going on.

He considers in that moment, however briefly, telling her exactly what has transpired over the past two days. She is his wife and she has a right to know. Not now, though. Not yet. He hasn't come to terms with the person he's become, what he has done over the weekend and what it has done to him. Telling her would be like telling a truth that wasn't yet his to share. Instead, he lies: If I knew, I would tell you.

Would you? Would you really fucking tell me?

He lies again. I would.

Bullshit. You never tell me anything. About your job. What you're feeling. All you talk about is your mother and how expensive it is to keep her alive.

He stands and tucks his shirt into his pants. I'm going to go now.

Where? Where are you going?

It's best you not know.

She sobs a little, wipes her nose with the back of her hand. She seems to accept him at his word this time. There is a sense of surrender in all of her small movements. What if they try to kill you? she asks.

He fastens the buttons on his shirt. I guess I'll try and kill them first.

But, she says. But what if—

I'm a police officer, he says. I've got my training. If someone pulls a weapon on me, I'll shoot them dead. He makes his finger and thumb into the shape of a gun, draws it quickly from his pocket, and points it at her. Then he makes a small gunshot sound, the tip of the finger-barrel raising as he does, and smiles weakly.

He goes to the bedroom and opens the drawer on his bedside table. Inside is his standard issue thirty-eight calibre revolver in its holster. He unbuckles his belt, pulls it through the loops of his pants, and slides the holster into place on his right hip. He takes extra ammunition from the box in the drawer and tucks it into the breast pocket of his shirt.

At the front door, he grabs a baseball hat from the top of the coat rack. His wife comes to the foyer and watches him. Be careful, she says.

Will do.

I love you, she says.

Before he opens the door, he takes her in. She is beautiful, too, and good. It pains him that he could never amount to anything close to that, anything deserving of the same particles and space and air. He lowers his head. Quietly, he leaves.

HANNAH FIELDS

S he is at her kitchen table, painting again, working on the
Monet scene she began the day before. Her head feels clear
for the first time today and the colours on her canvas appear lucid
and defined. She works on the first of the water lilies, their pink
pastel hues floating on the beginnings of the blue and green murk
of the pond. There is a confidence in her strokes that she did not
feel yesterday, has maybe never felt before. The patio door faces
west and the sun is low in the late afternoon, flooding the kitchen
with a tangerine light.

Her parents have not yet returned from the Sunsetter. This
is good, she thinks. She can come and go as she pleases from the
house without them harping on her to stay and rest. She looks
at the digital clock on the back of the stove. It reads 5:40 and she
knows she should leave soon. If he is going to meet her, to actually
take her up on her note, then she should beat him there.

The address she wrote down is for the abandoned gravel pit on
the south edge of town. It will be empty this Sunday, still early in

the evening, with the Sunsetter open for one final day and everyone either recovering from the night before or heading to the grounds for one last fix.

She doesn't have much of a plan for what she will do if and when the cop shows up. Only that she will bring the gun and the bullets and she will tell him that she knows what he did. The idea of going public with that information seems impossible to her—and he is probably aware of that, too. He is the law and in this city people respect that. They aren't especially inclined to believe young women who speak out against it. But it was the law that inspected the scene after Nick's death, that did the same after Dallan's, and they've had free reign to create whatever narrative was most convenient for them. There is no part of that process she still trusts.

Nobody is going to question them when they say Dallan's death was a suicide, not after what happened to his best friend, the weight of that being understandably devastating. On Monday, Brooks and Dallan will be on the lips of everyone in the county—if they aren't already—but the months will pass and the memories of them will pass too until they're only names spray-painted under an overpass or tucked into the pages of a dusty yearbook. She knows the case is already closed on Nick, whose name nobody here will ever know.

If it's the last thing she ever does, though, she will look that man in the eyes and tell him she knows the truth about what happened at the Sunsetter, and maybe that fact alone will be enough to keep him from sleep, from peace and satisfaction, for the rest of his living years. There would be some small amount of justice in that, at least.

She finishes painting all the small sections that require the colour she mixed, a pale rose that reminds her of the flesh of a freshly filleted trout. She places her brush in a cup of water and swishes it around to remove as much of the paint as she can, then stands and stretches in the bright streaks of orange from the newly setting sun.

Her body still aches from the collision in Thomas's truck, her head cloudy, drawn tight, but the pills make the pain manageable.

At the front door, she takes her jacket from the hook and pulls it over her arms. The revolver and bullets are still heavy in the pockets. She leaves out the front door and makes for her mother's sedan parked on the boulevard.

She drives until the buildings of downtown and the various residential subdivisions give way to the lonely warehouses and commercial properties whose parking lots teemed with white work trucks when she was so much younger. The south side of Perron isn't good for much anymore. A few auto-repair shops and construction suppliers still operate out of the area, but that's out of stubbornness, for the most part, on behalf of the old men who did well in the area's heyday and would only close up shop now for death or a late retirement.

There is a final road that marks the city proper. On one side are the empty buildings, with their broken windows and graffit-ied walls, and on the other is the gravel pit. The lock to the front gate has long been severed and so she idles her car and gets out to swing the rusted metal arm clear of the driveway. She drives through the dirt lot and parks her car behind a sheet metal shed, out of sight. She exits the vehicle, kicks the dry, cracked dirt with the heel of her shoe.

She walks around the large open warehouse, a hangar-like building with crimped aluminum walls, and heads for the gravel pit. It is as deep as it is wide, at least a football field's length. The walls of the pit are graduated into a series of flat circular levels like the risers of a colosseum or an ancient Roman theatre. The exposed stone is a greyish beige, dry and dusty from decades of exposure to the air. At the very bottom, though, she can see a pool of water reflecting the last blue of the clear sky and the ensuing embers of the day's end.

She picks up a rock and hurls it into the expanse. She tracks it for a while, but loses it as it descends into the emptiness. She hears it a few seconds later as it finally lands on one of the many sections of the wall below. The crack echoes back up to her in waves.

She's been here only once before, has never had much interest in the parties that happened on weekends while she was in high school. They always get busted up by the police, who do a routine check of the area late every Friday and Saturday night, and drinking in a crowd outdoors has never been her idea of a good time like it was for Dallan.

The one time she did go was to impress a boy. His name was Kyle McGrath and he was in her eleventh grade woodshop class. Her dad encouraged her to take the class, said everyone should know a little bit about working with their hands, and she ended up enjoying it, building a wine rack and turning a baseball bat on the lathe and constructing a two-storey birdhouse that still hangs, fastened to a poplar tree, in her family's backyard. Kyle had steady friends in the class and she ended up working at a table with their group. He never seemed to care that much about the work he did, shrugging off botched cuts and crooked nails, and that struck her younger self as a brave stance to take in the world.

He asked her to go to the party with him there at the gravel pit on the final week of classes and she agreed. It was a rare departure for her, to spend a night in the company of near-strangers, especially at the invitation of a boy. He didn't offer her a ride and so she went with two of her father's beers tucked in her jacket and walked the half-hour from her house alone through the eerie, near-abandoned industrial park. When she arrived, the pit was crawling with teenagers, over fifty of them drinking and shouting and throwing their empty bottles into the depths of the hollowed earth. Some even shot fireworks and Roman candles out over the dark hole and she remembers the smell of their sulphur, how they lit up the recess below in chemtrails of colourful light until they fizzled out part way to the bottom.

That night she found Kyle drunk and stumbling around the edge of the pit. She tried to talk to him, but he was much more interested in holding the attention of his friends, so much so that he ended up actually falling over the edge while pretending to trip in a clownish display, down onto the first level of the swirling road below. He broke his forearm, the shattered bone protruding red and jagged from his torn skin. The ambulance came and busted up the party and suddenly she realized that what he cared about was not, in fact, nothing, but only something that was of no significance to her at all.

She kicks another rock into the pit for Kyle, for his desire to be impressive among young men. It rolls across the spot where he fell all those years ago and then skips over the lip and out of sight. The only sure way to never be disappointed by another is to be alone.

She takes the revolver out of her pocket and stares down the site with one eye open. The barrel is smooth and straight. She lowers it and pulls the small latch with her thumb, pushes the cylinder open with her other hand, exposing the empty chambers. She rests the butt of the gun on her hip like her grandfather taught her and fishes a handful of bullets from her coat pocket. She slips them into the empty chambers, one by one, until the ends of the rounds stare back at her like six golden eyes.

From beyond the large warehouse, she hears a car pull into the lot. She clicks the cylinder back into place, spins it a full revolution, and then slides the revolver back into the pocket of her coat.

DEPUTY ARNASON

He has passed by the lot at least a hundred times on patrol, looking for parties to break up or menacing groups of teenagers to question on a slow night. Before he joined the force, it was on his way to and from his old job, based out of a boxy warehouse, tenantless for what must be nearly a decade now. He pulls into the dirt lot. He has the radio off and he can hear the ground shift and crunch under the tires of the car. At first appearance, the gravel pit is as it should be—abandoned and without trespassers. An uneasiness overcomes him and he shimmies his shoulder to stop his skin from crawling.

He drives at a slow roll through the lot, scans for the presence of the girl. His head still aches, a low moan in his temples, and the dehydration has manifested itself as steady pain in the muscles of his extremities, and also something deeper, more unsettling, in his abdomen.

His plan is to ask a few questions. He wants to seem normal, perfunctory to this young woman. After he goes through the cop routine, he'll try to find out what she knows specifically, and whether or not she's shared it with anyone else. After that, he thinks he'll probably kill her. It's an act that must grow lighter, become easier with repetition. He's gone through the possible scenarios for this rendezvous and evaluated each one on the basis of self-preservation and necessity. By his reckoning, all of them arrive at the same seemingly inevitable conclusion. What's another notch on his belt when everything else has gone to such profound shit?

He finally sees a sedan parked behind a shed to his right. He parks his car in the space beside it—a prime spot, a real prize of seniority, reserved for the boss or foreman when the gravel pit was still up and running. He gets out and peers into the parked vehicle. There is nothing of note in the driver or passenger seats, the back bench empty, no garbage or loose papers on the floor. He goes around and looks for any body damage or bumper stickers, but the car is pristine as far as he can see.

The sheets of undulating metal that cover the warehouse are weathered and rusted. He brushes his fingers against their coarse surfaces as he comes around the building and then stops beside the open door to peer inside. There are piles of gravel at the far end, left mostly unmoved for over a decade now. He can see where the last bucket scoop was taken and the trails of footsteps where kids have climbed up the shifting sand and rock after sneaking in at night. The office is dark, windows broken. He moves on.

Past the warehouse is the expanse of the gravel pit. He can remember truckload after truckload leaving from the yard, heading out to the various construction projects that popped up in and around Perron when the going was good. This feels like another life, when he was one of the people who made ends meet on this side of town. Now he's just the person who surveils what's left, the corpse of it. He misses the rumble of generators towed behind work trucks, the procedural work of cleaning pipes, the feeling after one of his crews finished up in a refinery and the surfaces of the scaffolding and floors and tanks were like-new again. It was not easy work, often boring and hard on the body, but it paid well, bought him a house and a car in his first two years out of high school. He used to make a living removing the grit from the world.

He advances towards the great opening in the earth and that's when he sees her at the edge, watching him. What he all but knew to be true is confirmed. It's the boy's friend, unmistakable to him, the girl from the night before. She's in a jacket and blue jeans and her hair is blowing in the breeze that gathers in the pit and skirts its surface and curls all around the dusty lot. His heart sinks and he begins to sweat. He did not expect to feel anything when he saw her, but her presence is a reminder of the agony he has wrought. He bites the inside of his lip as he approaches her.

He stops some feet away from her and twists his foot in the gravel and dust. Well, he says. He gestures with his arms out beside him.

She is silent.

I made it, he says. There is a dumb nonchalance to his delivery. He shrugs, gestures his palms upwards. You called this meeting. You got something you want to discuss with me?

There is that hatred in her eyes again, the same seething he saw at the copy shop. It is a look he couldn't have identified until today. But he's seen something like it on many instances—through the rearview mirror in the eyes of the perps cuffed in the backseat of his patrol car, in the dealers and deadbeats he's had to rough up for Durham. There is a limitlessness in her pupils. They seem to spill over the edge into her irises.

My name's Arnason—Deputy Arnason. You probably already know that.

I didn't, actually, she says flatly.

So far at least one of us has learned something, he says. I saw you took a liking to my mother—and my wife. Those were pretty pictures you left me on my doorstep. He pauses. I hate to ask, but

I'll come right out with it, I guess. What's with all those bullets you tossed in there? You scared the shit out of my wife.

Her mouth moves as if she is about to speak, but she hesitates.

I'm giving you a chance to say something here, Arnason says. So go on. Speak.

So she does. I know what you are, she says.

And what is that? One corner of his mouth cocks in an off-kilter grin. It sickens him that it does. He clenches his facial muscles, forces himself expressionless. What am I, exactly?

You're supposed to be a fucking cop.

I've got two jobs, he says. Sometimes they conflict in ways I don't have any control over. He thinks about the young man in the bog, the one he let off to make a run for it. He gave him that second chance, a hopeful epilogue to mistakes made.

You're pathetic, she says.

It's been a long time since he's had to endure the harsh words of a school-aged girl. It's like he remembers it—lemon in a paper cut, salt water on the skin exposed by a fingernail trimmed too short.

Nick, the girl says. He wasn't just some nobody.

He's surprised by this name. In all his jagged recollections of this weekend, he hasn't heard or seen it.

You know him, she goes on. The Sunsetter. Friday night. He hit his head. Dallan tried to make it right yesterday and you turned him away. You ignored him. You said Nick was nothing.

He closes his eyes and nods, remembers the conversation. The carnie kid, he says. He whacked his head, that's for sure. Besides that, I can't say much about it. I only know what I read from the report back at the station. I know your friend came in and told his story, but that's all we were ever going to see it as. A story.

Her facial muscles clench, lines deepening on her forehead. Her eyes are red and wet and full of wild anger. He is afraid of her, of the animal volatility in her eyes.

He puts his hand on the gun holstered on his hip. It seems to me we only have a couple options here, he says. One: I can kill you. But you don't want that and I don't know if I have the stomach for any more of this. The second option is that we both leave here today and you don't say another word about any of this to anyone. Ever. You forget this weekend happened and you go on and live your life. If you don't keep your mouth shut, you're dead. Days from now, years even. I don't care. My people will know. If it's not me that does the job, someone else will.

Exactly. What are you going to do about the others? she asks him.

What others?

That creep who was at the hospital this morning. Your boss. Everyone else you work with.

I'll take care of them. I'll make damn sure they don't lay a finger on you.

How?

Durham tried to make you a deal, didn't he? I've still got some pull, too. They'll leave you alone. You have my word.

She is a statue, this girl, save for the breath she inhales and exhales, making her chest rise and fall, and her hair lifting and ebbing in the gusts that rise from the pit. He can't even see her blink. Her face is flushed, but her eyes have dried again. He can see how young she is now, no older than twenty. He imagines her as a child, a smaller, softer version of herself, and then as a woman, his wife's age, in a home somewhere with a person she cares for, with a car she owns and a yard she tends to and furniture she probably doesn't even notice, working a job she loves or hates or feels nothing towards. And he recognizes once more that she feels the purest sort of hatred towards him—he knows this is true—and it haunts him to know that he, through the acts he has committed, has turned a person like her to such abject hate.

He has come to admire the conviction she clearly feels, one he thinks he can only barely conjure in some past version of himself, one that he maybe never even had. While he has felt remorse, true regret throughout the day and the night before, he is only now coming to understand what his role has been in the lives of others, lives like hers, in recent days.

He feels the breeze on his neck, a respite from the dry heat. The light is low. Magic hour, his wife has always called it. The time of day when the sun softens, filters through the horizon like a flashlight in campfire smoke. It casts no shadows. He looks at the girl and it occurs to him to smile at her. So he does. Then he gets down on one knee and takes up a handful of the grey dust and gravel. He wants to feel the coolness of the earth. It spills between his fingers, drying his palm and colouring it white like sweat on the band of a baseball cap.

He looks up from the ground and watches as the girl removes her hand from her jacket pocket, fast and calculated. She extends her arm, points a revolver at him, straight on and stock-still. She pulls the trigger.

HANNAH FIELDS

She walks over to him, stands above his body, his back in the dirt. She is completely calm, in full control of her extremities. A small line of blood trickles out of the single hole in his forehead, along the horizontal lines of his brow and onto the ground where it is soaked up by the dust. His eyes are wide and still, fixated on the clear orange sky above them both. She places her revolver back in her jacket pocket, then crouches down, eyes the gun still tucked in the holster at his side.

She is both like this man and not—a killer but also an agent of reckoning. She thinks of Nick and of Dallan, the goodness they embodied, and can't help but feel right in her convictions, though she knows the reality of what she has done will come on soon like a summer storm.

Her idea isn't without holes, she knows, but it's all she can think of in the moment. She reaches into her pocket and removes two paper napkins. With one hand, she unsnaps the strap holding the revolver in his holster, and with the other she pinches the stock of the gun and slides it free. She makes sure the paper is wrapped all the way around the stock, fits the other napkin into the guard over the trigger, and fires off a single shot down into the gravel pit.

She gets on one knee and fits the man's revolver into his own right hand, gently placing his finger on the trigger. She stands up and crumples the napkins into a ball, slips them back into her pocket. She drags her foot, levelling the grooves made in the gravel by her footsteps and knee. Then she turns her back on him and heads for her car.

†

In her basement, Hannah crouches down in front of the tall wooden cabinet. She fishes the key from under the marble chess set and unlocks the latch in the centre of the glass pane doors.

She opens the bottom drawer and takes out her father's cloth, kit, and solvent. She frees the cylinder, removes the bullets and the single spent brass casing, and looks down the barrel of the gun from the open chamber. On it, she can still smell the gunpowder residue. She undoes the buckles of the foldable plastic gun cleaning kit and removes a cylindrical brush, dips it in the solvent and cleans the inside of the barrel. With the cloth, she polishes the external metal, oils the wooden stock, and then lays her grandfather's gun down on the display cushion.

Upstairs, she goes to her room and pulls her largest backpack out from under her bed. It is made of heavy canvas, the flap and straps a worn brown leather. From her dresser to her closet to her nightstand, she collects what clothing and necessities she'll need, a photo of her family out at the farm, another of her late dog Scobey and the only postcard Nick ever sent: a black and white photo of Niagara Falls, the sun catching in its permanent mist, and a man in a barrel, caught in the current, exclaiming in cartoon letters, *I'm falling for you!*

In the washroom, she fills her toiletries sack with a toothbrush and toothpaste, a new stick of deodorant, tampons and all the tiny travel containers of soap, shampoo, and conditioner her mother has stashed away from various hotel stays.

There is a drawer in her father's dresser where he keeps a ceramic piggy bank nestled among all the old t-shirts he never wears. She takes it out and places it on the bed. With her fingernail, she pries open the rubber stopper on the pig's belly and shakes it over the comforter. First the smaller change tumbles out, followed by the bigger coins, and eventually the ten- and twenty-dollar bills that her father has stashed away inside, his rainy day fishing gear fund. She takes all of the bills in a stack and folds them into her wallet. She takes some of the change, too, and then returns what's left into the piggy bank, hides it back in the drawer.

†

She walks this time, taking the back streets that circumvent the centre of Perron, the ones she remembers riding her bike along as a child. The trees here have pushed up against the asphalt and concrete and long rounded masses have grown out of the surface of the road where the roots search for earth and water. They raise the sidewalk blocks in a series of lopsided platforms.

The backyards of these older houses are smaller than in the newer developments. The roofs of laneway garages slope, heavy with green moss and rotting deadfall. The dark of night has brought along a coolness and the trees and houses seem to sweat out the day's heat, earthy and damp.

She takes her time, her hands in the pockets of her jacket, the straps of her backpack digging into her shoulders. The closer she gets, the more she can hear. The Sunday night country bands bring less bass than the Friday and Saturday shakers, but the shrill steel strings of the acoustic guitars still carry in the night. The engines of the Tilt-a-Whirl and Zipper thunder their riders around and around, the Octopus's arms slice blade-like through the evening air.

She crosses the street to the chain-link fence, the unassuming physical barrier between the town and the Sunsetter, a world all on its own. She tosses her backpack over the top and climbs the fence, fitting the toes of her shoes in the diamond-shaped gaps between the wire. At the top, she swings her legs over, one after the other, and jumps down.

Her parents are likely in the beer tent listening to the bands. Probably everyone she knows is somewhere nearby right now. She can't be seen, so she walks behind the tents, along the lengths of thick power cables, around the gas generators and empty box crates. She takes this path westward past the Ferris wheel and Nick's old game booth with its black-and-yellow stripes until she emerges behind the midway in the rows of trailers belonging to the Carlsbad crew.

A pair of workers, a young man and middle-aged woman, are sitting in folding chairs outside an aluminum airstream trailer. They ash their cigarettes in a dish on the table between them and drink from brown glass bottles of beer. She approaches them.

Sorry, she says.

Nothing to be sorry about, the woman says.

You can't be back here, the young man says. His facial hair is sparse and stringy.

Shut up, the woman says. I'll be dead before you make any of the rules around here. She turns to Hannah. What are you looking for, hon?

I'm looking for a man named Del.

The young man and the woman exchange glances. Then the young man looks at his shoes and swallows a mouthful of beer.

Del'll be in his trailer, the woman says. His is the Jayco camper, last on the right.

Thank you, Hannah says.

Careful with Del though, the woman says. He can be a real prick.

Hannah smiles politely at the woman and walks away. There are more people out and about in the trailer park than the night before. Sunday night at the Sunsetter is never as busy as the Friday or Saturday and so she imagines a lot of Carlsbad crew members are having some downtime before they have to hustle and pack up late into the night in order to hit the road by morning.

There are patio lanterns, in all the primary colours, strung up along the awning of the Jayco trailer. A cardboard box filled with empty milk and beer bottles is at the bottom of the black retractable stairs. A mesh lawn chair is folded up, leaning against the wall.

She steps up to the camper door and knocks. At first there is quiet, but then she hears heavy steps inside. They draw nearer until finally the door swings open, barely missing her face, the breeze from it brushing the tip of her nose and fluttering her eyelashes.

The man inside is clean-shaven, his dark hair parted and pushed back with pomade. He wears a plaid shirt, the buttons done up right to the top, and a pair of clean blue jeans. He brings his hand to his chin and scratches at his smooth skin, cocking his head at her and raising one eyebrow. You lost? he asks.

Del.

He looks past her, now, and surveys the area around his camper with quick shifts of his eyes. Do I know you?

We've met. Last summer.

You look familiar.

I was hoping to talk to you.

About what?

She places one foot on the bottom step. About Nick.

He considers this for a moment. I was wondering if you might come by about him. He nods his head and waves her in.

The camper is organized, spotless even. The only signs that anyone lives in it are the few dishes stacked neatly on the drying rack over the kitchenette sink.

Take a seat, he says. Can I get you anything?

She shakes her head.

He offers her a spot on the couch by the door, goes and sits on the far bench seat behind the dining table that folds out from the wall.

She puts her heavy backpack down at her feet and crosses her legs. She stares straight at Del, waits for him to talk first.

I know who you are, he says. You've got to be Pretty's girl, the one he wouldn't shut up about.

This hurts her, though she wonders if it shouldn't make her glad.

We did meet, didn't we? he says. About this time last year.

We did, she says.

Look, I'm sorry for what happened to him. It may not look like it to a townie like yourself, but this can be dangerous work. Accidents, they happen.

It wasn't an accident, she says.

He shakes his head. I'm telling you, shit happens around here. He's not the first.

No, she says. It wasn't like that. She goes on. She tells him about Dallan, about what she saw behind the tents near the Ferris wheel. Then she mentions Brooks, how he died, how Dallan swore Nick sold them the drugs. This part seems to get Del flustered. He shakes his head repeatedly.

I don't know about any of that, he says. I'm telling you what the cops told me.

She has to get it all out. She tells him about Arnason, how she and Dallan saw him dig up the bag at the golf course and, later, Dallan seeing him make the drop off to Thomas's dealer. She talks about the night before, the way that Arnason killed Dallan only a matter of feet from his trailer where they are now, and how the sheriff was waiting in the hospital the next morning when she woke up.

Del sighs, scratches a little behind his ear. What a fucking mess, he says. He pulls himself up on the bench and rests his elbows on the table. And what about this cop, this Arnason? Does he know you're here?

She pictures him, eyes wide and blank, back in the dirt.

He doesn't, she says.

So what is it you want from me?

She takes a deep breath. I want a job. I want out of here. I want to work for you.

You don't want to work here. It's shit work. Really.

I can't stay in Perron, she says. This is the only way I see that happening.

I don't think so.

No, she says. She looks at him with all the confidence she's mustered through the day. I'm coming with you. You lost Nick. I'll take his job.

You've got to work your way up to that.

Fine then. I'll work my way up.

You'd have to start on the cleaning crew. It's not nice stuff, what they do.

I'll do it.

He folds his hands and rests his chin on them. How old are you?

Nineteen, she says.

Old enough, he says. What about your parents? By the looks of you, they don't know about this yet. I can't have a missing persons case on my hands.

I'll call them first thing in the morning. I promise.

He stands up and cracks his back. No. You go home and tell them, then you can come back first thing in the morning. We hit the road at dawn.

She shifts in her seat. Outside the screen door, the night is perforated by floodlights and the patio lanterns, small insects hovering about. She turns back to Del. I can't go home. I need a place to stay.

Stubborn, he says. He scratches again at his face, the beginnings of stubble barely visible along his jaw. Fine. You can have my trailer. I'll go shack up with one of the other bosses across the way. Del goes into the bathroom area, opens the medicine cabinet above the sink and collects a few things. I've been using the big bed there all weekend, but there's a couple of bunks behind you with fresh sheets. Help yourself to whatever. But get some sleep. Work starts tomorrow. Early.

†

She lies in the bunk. Sleep does not come easily. The distant music fades away and the calamity of the crowd is replaced by the shuffling of the busy feet and hushed voices of the Carlsbad workers outside the trailer.

She closes her eyes and there is nothing, no stars of the mind shimmering on the backs of her eyelids, no swimmers making ripples in the corners of this perfect, black expanse inside her head. She is reminded of a time she spent out east, at a lake far greater and deeper than any she had seen before it. Her aunt and uncle had a cabin there, before her uncle passed suddenly from pancreatic cancer and her aunt needed to sell the place, partially out of memories too painful for the property to be of any use to her anymore, but also to make ends meet.

Hannah remembers her bare back on the fine grey sand, the sound of the surf breaking on the boat launch, the smell of the water carried in with the breeze. She is alone on the beach in this memory, eyes closed, and she has just been called in for supper by her aunt. Before she can sit and join her family indoors, it's her aunt's rule that she has to rinse the sand from her body in the outdoor shower built on the back lawn.

On the beach, Hannah brings herself to stand, brushing off as many coarse granules as she can before going to wash them from her skin completely.

The door to the shower stall opens out to the lake and most days the surface is clear enough of people and boat traffic that you can look out while the spray falls onto your back. She heaves open the weathered wooden door, swollen and stubborn in the summer's humid heat, and on the floor of the shower she finds dozens, if not hundreds, of dead fish flies that have risen from the lake after laying their eggs before dying on all the roads and fields and patios of this place, to permeate the lives of its visitors and inhabitants, their corpses so common they become almost unnoticeable.

She brushes the area around the drain clear of their brittle wings and carapaces and turns the tap to start the water. She stands with her back to the yard, her face to the great lake. The surface is placid in the early evening and the water extends outward from the shore until it merges with the horizon in one all-encompassing grey.

Hannah Fields positions herself beneath the warm shower and washes it all away, the sand and sweat from her body, the flies from the floor that gather and swirl in the runoff collecting at her feet. Down, out of sight, through the open grate.

ACKNOWLEDGEMENTS

Thank you to my family, Ann, Marcel, Gabrielle, and Marc, for their love and support in all my writing endeavours, and to the Taters—Sue, Jeff, Monica, Meredith, and Madeline—for rooting for me, too!

Thank you to my agent, Akin Akinwumi, for believing in and championing this book. Your encouragement and fine eye were invaluable in its writing. Thank you to Dinah Forbes for your early editorial guidance.

To my editor, Jen Sookfong Lee, your enthusiasm and expertise breathed new life into this manuscript. Thank you to everyone at ECW, especially Jessica Albert, Jennifer Gallinger, Jen Knoch, Shannon Parr, Michela Prefontaine, Claire Pokorchak, Aymen Saidane, and Caroline Suzuki, for their efforts in making this novel a reality.

I am in constant admiration of my friends and my writing community. Shaun Robinson, Chris Evans, Mica Lemiski, Carter Selinger, Karina Palmitesta, Jessica Johns, Jocelyn Tennant,

Selina Boan, Brandi Bird, Rachel Jansen, Megan Jones, Kyle Schoenfeld—whether you offered comments on an earlier draft or helped me puzzle things out along the way, thank you.

Thank you to Chris Rogers for always spinning away on The Gravitron with me, and to my dad, who still loves the chuckwagon races.

Finally, thank you to my partner, Mallory. Without you, none of this is possible.

This book is also available as a Global Certified Accessible™ (GCA) ebook. ECW Press's ebooks are screen reader friendly and are built to meet the needs of those who are unable to read standard print due to blindness, low vision, dyslexia, or a physical disability.

At ECW Press, we want you to enjoy our books in whatever format you like. If you've bought a print copy just send an email to ebook@ecwpress.com and include:

- the book title
- the name of the store where you purchased it
- a screenshot or picture of your order / receipt number and your name
- your preference of file type: PDF (for desktop reading), ePub (for a phone / tablet, Kobo, or Nook), mobi (for Kindle)

A real person will respond to your email with your ebook attached. Please note this offer is only for copies bought for personal use and does not apply to school or library copies.

Thank you for supporting an independently owned Canadian publisher with your purchase!

This book is made of paper from well-managed FSC® - certified forests, recycled materials, and other controlled sources.